Ilene Grydsuk is a post-doctoral fellow with a research focus on biopsychosocial factors impacting personal well-being. She holds a PhD in public policy specializing in health services. She debuted as a science-fiction writer in 2022, earning an Editor's Choice, Reader's Choice, and Brew Book Excellence Awards and is a 2023 American Writing Awards Finalist. Ilene is a mother of three grown children and lives and writes on her ranch in Southern Ontario, Canada.

For Jay and Beatrice, thank you for always having my back, no matter what. I cannot imagine life without the unbreakable bond between us.

Ilene Grydsuk

REDEMPTION

The E.V. Chronicles Book 3

AUSTIN MACAULEY PUBLISHERS®
LONDON * CAMBRIDGE * NEW YORK * SHARJAH

Copyright © Ilene Grydsuk 2025

All rights reserved. No part of this publication may be reproduced, distributed, or transmitted in any form or by any means, including photocopying, recording, or other electronic or mechanical methods, without the prior written permission of the publisher, except in the case of brief quotations embodied in critical reviews and certain other non-commercial uses permitted by copyright law. For permission requests, write to the publisher.

Any person who commits any unauthorized act in relation to this publication may be liable to criminal prosecution and civil claims for damages.

This is a work of fiction. Names, characters, businesses, places, events, locales, and incidents are either the products of the author's imagination or used in a fictitious manner. Any resemblance to actual persons, living or dead, or actual events is purely coincidental.

Ordering Information
Quantity sales: Special discounts are available on quantity purchases by corporations, associations, and others. For details, contact the publisher at the address below.

Publisher's Cataloguing-in-Publication data
Grydsuk, Ilene
Redemption

ISBN 9798891559127 (Paperback)
ISBN 9798891559134 (Hardback)
ISBN 9798891559141 (ePub e-book)

Library of Congress Control Number: 2024916980

www.austinmacauley.com/us

First Published 2025
Austin Macauley Publishers LLC
40 Wall Street, 33rd Floor, Suite 3302
New York, NY 10005
USA

mail-usa@austinmacauley.com
+1 (646) 5125767

Chapter 1

'The boundaries which divide life from death are at best shadowy and vague. Who shall say where the one ends, and where the other begins?'
—Edgar Allan Poe

I stand in the makeshift doorway, my world falling away like sand sifting through an hourglass. I am too late. I don't even smell it anymore; my senses have gone numb. I can only stand here and stare. The flies are swarming him, defiling him.

I think I might be sick, the nausea roiling inside me like a ship tossed at sea. Achilles sits at my side, a quiet whimper escaping his throat. I once heard that nightmares are the psyche's way of processing our deepest fears. Score one for nightmares.

Jake is sleeping. Or is he? A sheen of sweat covers his brow, his skin an anemic grey. I didn't see it at first, but the soft pelt over his prone form is quivering. His whole body must be trembling under there. Achilles pads to Jake's side and turns to face me. What am I afraid of? It's Jake. Just as I take a step forward, he moans, shifting his position.

Hundreds, maybe even a thousand shimmery blowflies rise from the pallet. They move in formation, angry at the interruption. His left arm, the one tucked under his head just a moment ago, flops over the cover as he settles onto his back.

The stench hits me like a tsunami; if it was overpowering before, now it's unbearable. Either Achilles has no olfactory bulb at all or a tolerance for fetor that is beyond impressive. He sits quietly and patiently while I try to gain control of a runaway gag reflex.

I'm still working on keeping the bile from rising into my mouth when my eyes go wide. I've discovered the source of the necrotic nectar. Now that the horde of flies is airborne and he has changed positions, I see Jake's left arm for the first time.

As if to confirm my suspicion, the flies settle back down, concentrated on his left hand and forearm with stragglers landing at his elbow. Black veins protrude through thin leathery skin that seems to be weeping with infection. Ugly sores cover his entire hand and part way up his arm, oozing pus from just below his thumb. The flies are drunk on the putrescence.

The wolf sniffs at the offensive appendage, the fur on his hackle's bristles, he curls his lip in a threatening snarl. He pads around the pallet, head low, scenting the air, eyes searching.

I whisper, "What is it, boy? Is it still here?"

He ignores me for a moment and then, as if in answer, the fur at the back of his neck flattens out, the grimace on his face falls away. He walks back to me, more like a dog now than a predator, signaling that we are out of danger. For now.

I stand in stunned silence, trying to take in the enormity of the conundrum. I look down at Jake. There is one thing I know for sure. The last time the beast attacked Jake, he wanted to wield him like a weapon. This time, he just wants to kill him.

Pedro's lids protest, the best he can do on his first attempt is capture his own eyelashes catching the sun. Disoriented and incoherent, his vision blurs when he tries to look beyond them. Numbness permeates throughout his body making him wonder if it is still attached. He must be dead. Wait. A tinny voice to his right, speaking his native tongue.

"*Ele acorda.*" He wakes.

Does this mean he is alive? The last thing he remembers with any degree of clarity is running the scalpel through Draeger's back. And the smear of the deadly toxin on his thumb. He doesn't feel incarnate, not exactly. More like a disembodied spirit, floating on the wind. He feels, nothing. A hazy shadow enters his field of vision.

He squints and works on focusing. Behind the shadow, he sees the object blocking the light. A large hand, a man's hand, fingers as gnarled as a Krummholz tree, parchment paper skin with a yellowish tinge, and thick, brittle fingernails that are more calcified than keratinized.

The hand hovers over his face. He tries to lift his arm and swat it away, to no avail. A soft voice whispers in his ear. He can feel the faintest pressure as another hand presses against his arm, holding it down.

"*Não*. He is a friend. The medicine man will help you."

Pedro squints harder, willing his eyes to cooperate. A soft face comes into quasi-focus, framed by long raven tresses. A sash of red paint crosses over artesian cheekbones and a small celestial nose, stretching from temple to temple. It is only a momentary distraction from captivating mocha-colored eyes accentuated with kohl wing tips. An ornamental headdress made from bright turquoise dyed feathers completes the picture, a crown befitting that regal face.

He tries to formulate words, they come out in a sottish slur.

"Whoooru? Whurmi?"

The voice giggles just a little, the sound tilting away from his ear, "*Avô*, I think he has had enough cordoncillo."

His brain picks up bits and pieces of the message; *avô*, Grandfather, cordoncillo? His scientific mind elicits an image of a wilted looking shrubbery. It would explain his inability to form words and his general anesthetic state. That silky black hair dances in his face once again as the voice speaks directly in his ear.

"You are safe. You are on Tapeba land now, among the Tupi people. No one will harm you here. I am called *Sol da Manhã*, tribal chief. This is my grandfather, *Anda na Chuva*, Tapebano healer. *Árvore Errante* and Tank found you while out hunting."

The words swirl around in Pedro's head, out of order at first, the effort it takes to sort it out brings a bead of perspiration to his upper lip. Tapeba land, Tupi tribe. Safe. *Sol da Manhã*, Morning Sun, Chief. *Anda na Chuva*, Walks in the Rain, Medicine Man. *Árvore Errante,* Wandering Tree. Hunting. *Tank.* Tank?

Morning Sun's beautiful face disappears. A new one takes its place. This one with a bass voice so deep it vibrates in his chest.

"Tank did all the work. He smelled the blood."

The biggest head he has ever seen, a giant's head. The hand that rests on his shoulder swallows the whole left side of his body. Suddenly his name makes sense. Wandering Tree whistles and an equally impressive canine comes bounding into view, a Brazilian Mastiff the size of a pony. Dark brindle coloring, long jowls and floppy ears that swing in harmony as he trots forward, skin folds that extend into powerful shoulders.

The dog sniffs the air as he approaches and looks to his master who beckons him forward with a quick click-click of his tongue. Tank. The dog stands over Pedro's prone form, no malice in his eyes as he considers him.

Walks in the Rain speaks for the first time, his voice gruff with age, his authority incontrovertible.

"Enough. He needs rest. *Árvore*, fetch the *Sangre de Drago*, I must prepare more salve. It must be re-applied to the wound."

Wandering Tree and Tank make to leave. Pedro is drawn to the massive dog. He lifts his right arm to stroke the soft coat. Shock followed by a cascade of flashbacks pulls Pedro under as he watches a stump rise into the air where his hand used to be.

Father is pacing the length of the sick room, pondering. The fever claws at the edges of Draeger's consciousness. He grits his teeth, flexes every muscle, at least the ones he can still feel, desperate to stay alert. Father hates weakness. His patriarch stops wandering, snaps his long, slender fingers and looks to the doorway. Not a minute passes before a servant knocks softly.

"Enter," Father summons in his imperial tone.

A diminutive wraith of a girl appears; long black braids on either side of an angelic face, deep-set almond-shaped eyes, smooth, flawless skin, a delicate nose and a small mouth with generous, rounded lips.

It was such a delightful surprise to acquire this one, from the ancient Ming dynasty no less. Her bloodlust is legendary, even here, after centuries in purgatory. She bends on one knee and bows low the second she enters. Father does not wait for her to rise.

"Chinda, I am in need of a physician. A specialist in chemical injury. Tell me we have a condemned soul with these skills."

Chinda is still on bended knee. No one disrespects Father.

"Rise, Chinda," Father adds impatiently.

The girl stands, she barely comes to Father's chest at full height. Her miniature frame is swaddled in an elegant silk kimono in a resplendent emerald color. A melodic voice that reminds Draeger of a siren addresses Father.

"Yes, my Lord. I have the perfect candidate in mind. Give me but five minutes."

Father dismisses her with an absentminded wave. He resumes pacing as the door closes behind Chinda.

True to her word, she returns, closer to three minutes later, with a lecherous-looking man in his early 50s, wearing a white lab coat. Even in his present state, it is not hard for Draeger to imagine his earthly sins. He watches Chinda in the same way a half-starved coyote watches a hare.

His manners have not improved since taking up residence in Father's realm; Chinda kicks him in the back of the knees, perhaps a little too forcefully, when he fails to show fealty. Draeger winces inwardly. Father will repay this slight, if not now, then when the sap is least expecting it. Father never forgets.

"My Lord. This—" her lip curls upward in disgust as she glances over at him, "is Doctor Sanstrom. He is, was, quite a renowned clinical toxicologist in his past life. Before his extracurricular endeavors with unsuspecting patients led to his untimely demise."

And a one-way ticket to perdition.

Father does not seem amused. He taught Draeger at a very young age that not all sin is created equally. Take Chinda, for example. A ruthless assassin to be sure, but her acts carried out in servitude to her orphan emperor. There is a certain respectability to her crimes. By comparison, this scoundrel is barely human.

Draeger's eyes flutter to the offensive man at her side, the lust in his eyes hardly contained. Father's tone is dripping with contempt when he finally addresses the doctor.

"Approach the prince," he indicates Draeger's prone form. "I must learn of the cause of his current state, and more importantly, how to reverse it."

Never one to curry favor, Draeger knows what it costs Father to ask for assistance. Sanstrom is downright flippant in his response.

"Well, I might be able to diagnose his condition. For a price."

He looks Chinda up and down with a leer.

The impudence of the address, the arrogance in Sanstrom's tone as he addresses the Erinyes, the King of Hell, makes him shrink back. Even in his semi-delusional state, Draeger can feel the change in ambience. Father is cross, yet Sanstrom stands, arms crossed with a smug look on his face, waiting to cut a deal.

"Very well, Dr. Sanstrom. First, the diagnosis. And the cure. And then…" Father does not finish.

Sanstrom's smile turns predatory as he sweeps greedy eyes once more over Chinda and laughs.

"I knew it the minute I walked in the room," he says as though even an imbecile would know the answer. "The tells are so obvious," he huffs with an exaggerated eye roll.

He pokes at Draeger's arm lying stiffly at his side, lifts it, and then lets it drop unceremoniously. He repeats the callous gestures with Draeger's legs and then turns to Father.

"See here?" he points to a tiny ripple on the skin of Draeger's forearm. "And here?" Another on his right calf. "Muscle spasms."

He lifts the right leg anew and lets it drop again. "And this? The rigidity, the woodenness of the limbs. He can't feel them you know. He is paralyzed. It's classic symptomology."

Sanstrom looks positively triumphant as he finishes his diagnosis.

"He's been poisoned by a dart frog. Judging by the degree of rigor mortis, or pre-mortis, I would say the golden dart frog is probably the culprit."

Draeger registers the words. He was right, amphibious. Father nods, obviously thinking the same thing.

"And the anecdote, Dr. Sanstrom," Father asks in a flat cadence.

"There is none," Sanstrom says simply.

The room goes dim, the flames in the sconces on the walls flickering almost to extinction. Sanstrom clears his throat, the first sign of discomfort since his arrival today. He offers more information.

"Well, the golden dart frog does have one natural enemy, but I don't know how this is helpful. There is only one animal that eats the frog, it has unusual saliva that neutralizes the batrachotoxin."

Draeger catches a glimpse of Father in his peripheral vision, unmoving, unblinking, arms crossed.

"Oh, for pity's sake!" Sanstrom obviously thinks this is a waste of time. "It's the *leimadophis epinephelus,* most people just call it the fire-bellied snake."

Chapter 2

'Health is not valued till sickness comes.'

—Dr. Thomas Fuller, 1732

Maureen Domanso marches the length of the conference room, back and forth, wearing a pathway into the carpeting. Draeger has been gone for over a week now. He has not made contact and she has no idea where he is. Or why he left. As she retraces her footsteps over and over, she begins to doubt herself. Did she make the right call suggesting the coup?

Perhaps one of the cabinet members went straight to Draeger with her plan. Perhaps he is plotting his counterattack right now. She shudders at the thought of what he might to do her for retaliating. Or what the existential virus has in store for her for her chicanery. And yet…she feels hale and hearty, better than she has in many months.

She pulls up the latest reports, her hunch about Draeger losing control of EV all but a certainty now. The virus is behaving as she has for over one hundred years, save the for last one. Minor righting protocols for personal indiscretions, more as remnants of the recent unrest than anything.

She eyes each minister wearily as the agents enter the conference chamber, looking for any signs of duplicity. All she sees are fuller, brighter faces, lustre beginning to return to skin and hair, newfound energy in their movements as they make their way to their respective seats. She can almost feel the relief wash over the room as the agents realize that Dr. Draeger is not in attendance.

When everyone is settled, Maureen steps to the head of the long table and addresses the group.

"Well then, don't you look a whole lot better than the last time we met. We all seem to be recovering remarkably well. Any regrets?"

Head shakes all around.

"My only regret is not doing it sooner," Janet Eams quips, eliciting a few chuckles.

"But, what about Dr. Draeger?" the youngest member of the group asks. "Won't he know what we've done?"

The room goes very still. The mention of Draeger is an arresting thought.

"Let me worry about that," Maureen replies. "In the meantime, let us recap our progress since we last spoke."

As the agents report one by one, Maureen can almost feel the tide shifting. The embargos and moratoria have been lifted, expropriation of goods has halted, onerous production quotas eliminated, the heavy-handed administration abolished.

Civil unrest and social decay are already reversing course. And still, Draeger doesn't seem to have noticed. He is obviously preoccupied with something else at the moment. Of what, Maureen does not know, but she plans to use the time and space his diversion has afforded her to keep it that way.

The silence is deafening. Sandra and Gordon sit on the living room sofa, the seat cushion a chasm between them. Sandra's mother rests in the rocker to her left, her gentle swaying the only movement in the room. Evander is upstairs, he retreats after dinner like clockwork since that day. The day Sandra's life lost all meaning.

A swashbuckling action-adventure film plays on the television, the volume so low it might as well be muted. No one is watching anyway. Sandra keeps replaying it over and over in her mind, on a loop. It never fits, no matter how many times her brain repeats. What could Everett possibly have done to earn a righting protocol that would take her life?

Perhaps if any of this made sense, she could eventually make peace with it. But not left like this, with so many unanswered questions, so many missing pieces. It is eating her alive. The grief is overwhelming on its own, add the illogicality of it and it's just too much. Sandra will not, cannot, accept that the correction was a natural response to a grave transgression. It feels so very wrong.

Gordon tried consoling her, she nearly took his head off. She feels badly, he was only trying to help, but there is nothing worse than having someone else's rationalization thrust upon you as truth. At least her mother recognized her volatility and didn't try to justify Everett's passing.

She knows she has to pull it together, for her family, for her son. But something keeps gnawing at the edge of her conscience, egged on by her own righting protocol that never should have happened. She knows, on some deeper level within herself that there is more to this.

Sandra sighs, reaching for Gordon's hand but stopping partway. The gulf is still too wide. Without a word, she heads upstairs, passes Evander's room, and pauses at the doorway to her daughter's bedroom. Taking a deep breath, Sandra opens the door and slips inside.

After being sterilized, the room was returned to its original state, as though waiting for Everett to come home. She walks to the closet, swings it open and closes her eyes, taking in the scent of her first-born child still lingering on the clothes hanging neatly along the wall.

She walks to the bed, runs her hand along the soft blue duvet, sits on the edge and stares. Everett's cell phone sits exactly where she left it, charging on the nightstand. There was never a need to monitor her daughter's interactions, no need to worry about who she conversed with, how she spent her allotted time, an unfortunate preoccupation of ancient parents in a world gone mad.

Now she reaches for the phone, more to hold onto something, to feel some connection. The screen comes to life when she lifts the phone. No password protection or encryption in the new order, EV ensures propriety for all.

Tears roll down her face as Sandra scrolls through her camera roll. Everett at school with Jenny, smiling over Matt Colby's shoulder, at the park playing ball with her friends, Cosmo and Minx, her mother and father and brother. Then more recent photos. Of her daughter and a boy, a boy she does not recognize.

A ruggedly handsome young man with a shag of dirty blond curls, broad shoulders, an easy-going aspect. It looks like they are in a forest clearing. Sandra does not recognize the setting.

Photo after photo of the boy. Smiling, sticking out his tongue at the camera, funny faces, and then, more intimate images as he looks at the lens. At Everett. Who is this boy? Why did Sandra not know about this boy?

She flashes back to snippets of conversation from the funerary service. She recognized, well, everyone. Besides the family, her classmates from her graduating class, a slew of agents from the Department of Animal Welfare, even Dr. Pines and Dr. Viscov, Everett's supervising agents.

There were whispers, of course, speculation about what crime Everett had committed. How bad it must have been. No one knew. And then she recalled a comment from Matt Colby.

"Where is that Jake guy? I thought they were way more than friends anyway."

And then Toby, "True, where is Jake, what was his name again?"

"Domanso," Jenny filled in for the boys. "And yes, they were close. It's weird that he's not here."

Sandra rolls that little conversation around in her head, staring at the boy in the pictures.

"Jake Domanso, is it?" she says to the phone.

She sets the phone back down and stands, straightens out the duvet cover and heads for the door.

Time for a chat with Jake.

I see it now that Jake has shifted position. The hand hanging off the pallet, just below the thumb on the fleshy part of his palm, puncture marks. So red, the margins blend to black. I can almost see the path of the venom crawling up his arm along the veins, bruised a deep purple all the way to the elbow. My heart is pounding in my ears. I failed. Again.

Achilles whimpers beside me then takes my shift in his mouth and pulls back gently. I look down at him, our eyes locking. He repeats the motion, sniffing at the oversized pockets.

Pockets filled with leaves and roots and strange fruit. Not food, Achilles made that clear. I pull out a duck-shaped leaf, then a purple jellyfish flower, the wolf's eyes brighten as he looks from my hands to Jake and back.

Not food. Medicine?

A jolt of adrenaline renders me giddy. Maybe it's not too late.

I fly into action, emptying the contents of my pockets onto a makeshift table and begin sorting. Find a bowl Jake fashioned from a coconut shell, rush outside and rustle around the roots of the tree until I find a large round stone.

My mortar and pestle. I've watched Dr. Pines make poultices for the horses a half dozen times by now, the one difference being that I have no recipe. I look at the table and decide more is better.

I start adding leaves and stems, bark and flowers to my bowl, grinding them together with fierce determination. I grab one of the smooth round fruits to add to my concoction when Achilles growls softly.

"No? Not this one?" I ask the wolf. "Why not? You did make me take it from the grove didn't you?"

He growls again, a little more forcefully this time.

Okay, I think to myself. *No time to argue, especially with a 160-pound sabre wolf.* I set the fruit aside.

When my antivenom compress is as puréed as I can manage it, I approach Jake. Another moan escapes his lips, followed by a scrunching of his nose, as though he can smell his own sickness. Which wouldn't be hard to do. My own stomach rebels as I get closer, the scent of decay filling my nostrils making my eyes water and the back of my throat fill with bile.

I study the injured arm, the venom is not quite to the elbow yet, either it's really slow-moving, or the bite was interrupted before the tetra could deliver a fatal dose. The venom is certainly lethal, Jake's life force is fading. He's hanging on, but barely. Maybe, just maybe.

I return to the bowl, a liquid layer now sitting on top of the paste. Achilles looks at me expectantly. He wants me to, do what? He noses the bamboo cup on the floor by Jake's pallet. Got it. I pick up the cup and siphon off the liquid from the bowl.

Achilles approves. He rolls the strange fruit with his snout, bringing it to the cup. Yes, he is officially the most intelligent animal I have ever met. I'm pretty sure he's in charge.

I pick up the fruit, skewer it with a sharp stick and squeeze the juice into the cup. All I have to do is get Jake to drink it. Easy peasy. First things first, I get to work on the arm. The one currently teeming with hairy bionic bugs. Right. My tongue thickens at the back of my throat as if daring me to try for a deep breath.

I ignore the light-headedness that accompanies my shallow respirations as I lean in and disturb the roiling mass with a jerky wave of my hand. There, I can make out the source of Jake's misery.

As I am about to apply the poultice to the bite, I make a split-second decision I hadn't even contemplated until this moment. I think I saw it in a cheesy movie once. It might not help, but I am willing to try, despite the revulsion I feel at the thought of what I am about to do. I shoo again, then, using the sharp stick, I wiggle it into the fang marks, opening the wound.

Jake writhes, a good sign, he can still feel it. I pinch my nostrils once and then bring my mouth to the wound sealing my lips around the punctures as tightly as I can and then, I suck.

Fluid fills my mouth; it tastes like rancid apple juice. I know it won't hurt me, venom is not poison after all, but it sends a wave of panic through me anyway. I spit violently onto the floor. Again. I try one more time, the liquid, just a dribble now.

It seems I have created a new repast; I watch the flies settle into the mess on the dirt floor, gorging on the fetid liquid. My stomach threatens to upend itself again. The bloated tissue in Jake's hand and lower arm is visibly deflating.

Somewhat satisfied that I've relieved the pressure at least, I apply a generous helping of the muddy green plaster to Jake's hand and set the bowl aside.

Lifting his head, it takes considerable effort to keep it from lolling to the side, but I manage, I bring the cup to his lips, pouring small swills into his mouth. He swallows by reflex, tiny rivulets escaping the corners of his mouth and dripping down his chin. Still, he is ingesting more than he is dribbling.

I empty the cup; I've saved enough plant material to make more. Gently, I set Jake's head down, make sure he's not going to choke on any residual liquid, and when he settles back into sleep, I head to the stream to rinse the stomach-churning taste from my mouth.

Achilles stands and follows me out to the stream; I think we are both thirsty for fresh air. A niggling thought fleets across my conscience as we approach the stream. It seems I've been asleep an awfully long time. This dream is going on forever.

She knows she is playing a very dangerous game but Maureen is not deterred. She falsifies the latest monthly reports, changing raw data and then regenerating graphs and summary narratives that will appeal to Dr. Draeger. Hardly a new way of doing things, only this time, the tables are turned. The deceiver becomes the deceived. Disinformation, misinformation, misrepresentation; all ancient specialties wielded with Machiavellian panache in a, *say anything to get what you want* world.

She closes her computer screen and turns to face Peter, reclining on the sofa, the volume on the television turned low. He is snoring lightly, his lower lip gone slack, Hercules curled up against his slippers. At least in sleep, the worry lines that are now permanently etched on his face have slipped into temporary remission.

As she heads to her bedroom to prepare her nighttime ministrations, she ponders. It is odd that EV has not corrected her. Lies, insincerity, trickery even. There can be but one reason why she is being spared. The Biodome is sending her a clear message.

Stop him.

Now the question becomes, where the devil is he?

Chapter 3

'It is time now for us to rise from sleep.'
—Benedict of Nursia AD 480–AD 548

Father and Chinda turn Draeger onto his side, exposing the deep laceration on his back. He doesn't really understand what is happening, only that Father seems rejuvenated. The skepticism in Sanstrom's voice is dangerously close to insolence to Draeger's ear.

"I don't know what you hope to achieve here. I already told you, there is nothing to be done."

Father ignores him. He brings his perfectly manicured hands to Draeger's back. Draeger can faintly make out the whisper emanating from Father's lips. Soft, subdued, he can't decipher it.

The whisper becomes a chant, and then Father speaks, a clear command.

"Come my little *Liophus*, your master summons."

Initially confused, Draeger replays the exchange between Father and Dr. Sanstrom in his head. Reasoning is slow to come, his brain addled with infection. This much he knows; Father will not concede. He could not be more right.

"Now Chinda," Father orders.

Chinda moves like a cat, pouncing, a death sickle in each hand, two razor-sharp crescent moons sharpened to deadly points, the grip and pommel made to fit perfectly in her delicate hands. Before Draeger knows what is happening, he is flat on his stomach, Chinda straddled on his back facing his feet, rounded hook blades encircling each of his wrists, pinning them to his sides, the tips of the sickles embedded deep in the mattress. She applies an uncomfortable downward pressure.

"Ready my Lord," is all she says.

He doesn't see them, but his stomach convulses when he hears Father.

"Feast my brethren."

They are small, at least that is a mercy. Three fire-bellied snakes. Magnificent red scales running in stripes across the back and along the underbelly, they slither onto Draeger's back and into the slit along his spine left by a poisoned scalpel.

Draeger screams, writhing under Chinda. Slight though she may be, her strength is remarkable. The sickles hold, pinning him in place like a bug. Fire crawls up his spine into his brain stem, through his pelvis and down his legs, a scourge devouring him from the inside. Physically exhausted as he is, still he thrashes, and still Chinda vanquishes his protestations.

Father is at his ear now, an uncharacteristic softness in his tone, "It is almost over now son."

Draeger feels the urge to retch, his stomach spasming, diaphragm constricting violently. His mouth opens involuntarily, and one by one, three satiated fire-bellied snakes crawl from his oral cavity and slither into the darkness.

A gasp of surprise from Chinda, and then she springs off his back retracting her blades, like extensions of her hands. He feels a tightening around the slit in his skin. A strange sensation but he cannot place it. He cannot see the rigid crimson scales that spread out like a fan around the opening, replacing what was once human flesh.

Pedro unwraps the stump, examining the amputation. The oedema is not excessive and the is no sign of necrosis. In fact, it is already beginning to shrink. Walks in the Rain is very good.

Carefully, he replaces the bandages, the cauterized tissue is still susceptible, although a pinkish color is beginning to bloom at the margins of the burnt flesh. Pedro thanked his God for the 10th time that he was unconscious while the healer worked on his arm.

Morning Sun approaches, she reminds Pedro more of a schoolgirl than a tribal chieftess. They are of the same age; he finds it hard to imagine how she ascended to chief so early in life. She is demure in his presence, the warrior in her temporarily subdued.

"You are well, *Senhor*?"

Pedro harumphs, "As well as can be expected, I suppose, given my newfound disability."

He raises his handless arm in the air for emphasis.

Morning Sun raises an eyebrow.

"Feeling sorry for yourself, are you?"

Pedro sighs, "I suppose I am."

"Well, *Mão Roubada,* I don't know why, I think you look like a fierce warrior."

Morning Sun's bronze cheeks take on a distinctly rosy tone.

"*Mão Roubada?* Stolen Hand?" Pedro chuckles flailing his stump in the air. "Fitting."

"Wandering Tree thought so too." Morning Sun looks over at the behemoth frolicking with the equally enormous Tank.

She looks like she wants to say more but holds her tongue. Walks in the Rain is watching the exchange from his seat on a log bench at the edge of a fire pit. His hands never stop whittling the thick walnut branch in his lap, little pieces of shavings flying off with each pass of his sharp blade. He projects his voice without changing positions.

"I will ask for you, *Sol da Manhã,*" reading his granddaughter's thoughts. "Why were you so far out, alone, what was your purpose? And how did you come to lose your hand?"

Pedro stiffens, all light-heartedness evaporating like water poured over hot stones. He fumbles for an explanation, looks into Morning Sun's open face, genuine concern painted on her brow replacing the red stripe from yesterday.

The ceremonial headdress has been supplanted with a single black feather woven into a long tight braid. Without the headdress and red pigment ensconcing her delicate features, she is transformed from warrior to seraph. Pedro cannot bring himself to lie to her.

"I was not alone."

This gets the medicine man's attention. He slowly places his carving work on the bench beside him and hobbles over to Pedro. Morning Sun looks confused.

"What do you mean, not alone?"

She looks to the giant.

"Wandering Tree did not find anyone else with you."

The big man nods in confirmation.

Pedro stammers for a moment and then blurts, "That's because I killed him."

Morning Sun takes a step back from Pedro. He feels a squeeze on his heart at the gesture but continues.

"He is, was, a bad, bad man. He was hurting people. He…he, killed my mentor."

Morning Sun looks at him now as if for the first time.

"Why not let the existential virus punish this fiend? Now, you have cursed yourself!"

She looks at her grandfather for affirmation.

"You don't understand. He was controlling the virus, using it for his own gain."

Morning Sun is about to protest again when Walks in the Rain lifts his chin. The words die on her lips. The medicine man speaks slowly, carefully now.

"There is but one who could do such a thing."

He nods slowly while Morning Sun and Wandering Tree furrow their brows simultaneously. This is news to them too.

"Where did this killing take place, *Mão Roubada*?"

Pedro looks at each of them in turn, the three Tupi tribespeople watching him intently, unblinking. Even Tank is sitting still at Wandering Tree's side.

"It is hard to explain. We were on the Ceará Plateau and then, then we weren't. I followed him you see; he was looking for—" Pedro hesitates, hoping to avoid having to elaborate on this point. "Something he lost."

Walks in the Rain urges him on with only his eyes.

"He led me into a strange place. I have never seen anything like it. The vegetation changed from desert shrubs to the most peculiar undergrowth I have ever seen. It became dark, the air felt heavy in my lungs. Then we came to the rock face."

He shivers involuntarily at the memory of the corpse flowers and the buzz of carrion flies and the stink.

"There was an opening in the face, a cave. He went inside. I followed him and…I plunged my blade, my poisoned blade, deep in his back. Then I pushed him into a black void. I killed him. And my punishment for this wicked deed," he lifts the stump. "I poisoned myself."

Morning Sun has the look of someone who has just been slapped. Wandering Tree is petting his dog in even strokes down the animal's powerful back, his expression not giving away his inner thoughts. Walks in the Rain is shaking his head almost imperceptibly from side to side, his eyes never leaving Pedro's face.

After a deafening silence that stretches on and on, the elder wise man speaks, a hint of veneration in his tone.

"You have been to the Land of Crooked Shadows, *Mão Roubada*. Where man does not belong. You have killed no one."

Pedro perks up, eyebrows shooting into his hairline. Is the medicine man trying to ease his conscience? He is not burdened by what he has done, he does not regret it. He looks at his arm, this will be a constant reminder of what he sacrificed to rid the Biodome of Vladimir Draeger.

"*Si*, it is okay, *Anda na Chuva*, it had to be done. The man brought malevolence to the Biodome."

The medicine man purses his lips and shakes his head again, seemingly resigned.

"*Não jovem*, you killed no one. For the one who walks the Land of the Crooked Shadows cannot be killed."

Pedro looks to Morning Sun and then to Wandering Tree. They look as confused as he is. Walks in the Rain stands and turns to walk away. Just before he sets off, he looks to the sky and then directly at Pedro.

"You cannot kill the one who is already dead."

I must have rinsed my mouth out eight times, passed a bristly twig over my teeth at least as many times, and am currently chewing on a sprig of mint leaves. It feels like I've scrubbed the first layer of skin, maybe two, off my hands. I want to jump in the water, but I need to get back to Jake.

As Achilles and I make our way back from the stream, the sun is just beginning to set in the west. The giant orange orb teetering on the horizon is breathtaking, I slow to marvel at its beauty. My ever-patient companion matches my pace, seemingly content to be in my company.

The crickets are just starting their evening symphony when we reach the tree. The stench of decay lingers, but I think it has lost some intensity. A spark of hope blooms from deep inside me. When I pass through the vine curtain, the spark is smothered. Jake is lying in the same prone position, still unmoving.

With trepidation, I step closer, my eyes going wide as I see subtle changes, even in the dimming light. For one, the wet curls at his temple are drying. Yes, he still sleeps, but he looks somehow tranquil, like a calmness has washed over him. His coloring has improved, no longer the sallow patina of imminent death, but a more natural hue. And the abominable little robot flies are starting to disperse, losing interest in Jake's battered arm.

I spring back into action, working through the blur of tears. Squeeze the fruit, mix up a new elixir, bring it gingerly to his lips. Mash more flowers and leaves and roots, carefully wipe away the old and re-apply the new poultice to his injured hand. I move his arm into the waning light, yes, the black is receding. My heart leaps.

I settle on the floor beside Jake, Achille sidles in and curls up at my side. Now we wait. My eyelids grow heavy, I am being lulled by the rhythmic twitter of crickets. I find myself leaning into the wolf's thick white coat. He doesn't seem to mind one bit. Just as I am drifting off, I realize I don't think I've ever fallen asleep while I am already asleep. A dream within a dream, who knew?

Peter and Maureen Domanso look up at the same time, neither expecting the knock at the front door. Hercules lifts his head, his ears perking straight up, nose turned toward the entrance of the house. Peter wipes his hands on the dish towel and pats the dog on the head.

"It's okay boy, stay."

Maureen resumes stirring her coffee, then turns to rest her backside against the counter as her husband makes his way to greet the surprise visitor. Probably just a neighbor needing to borrow some milk or sugar, even Maureen has done this a time or two. When Peter doesn't return to the kitchen, she begins to question her own assumption.

She places her steaming cup on the countertop and heads for the front door when she spots him in the hallway, a woman following on his heels. She looks oddly familiar, but Maureen can't quite place her. She must have seen her walking her dog or working in her garden.

She guesses they are about the same age, too old to have young ones but not quite old enough to be a grandmother. Definitely familiar. The woman looks up at Maureen, a weak smile that doesn't even come close to reaching her eyes forced onto her pretty face. Peter's apprehension as he introduces their guest is palpable.

"Mare," he hesitates on her nickname, "this is Sandra. Sandra Steele. She has a few questions for us."

Maureen blanches at the last name as her autonomic nervous system commandeers her insides. It falls into place; she knows exactly where she's seen this woman before. First, from her DFO presentations at the annual conferences, her eco-restoration projects. But more than that. Her daughter is a dead ringer for her mother.

She tries for nonchalance, hiding her recognition. She musters her haughty public persona that most agents find intimidating.

"Ms. Steele, how can I," she looks to her spouse, "we, be of assistance?"

Now that she is close, the tells of Sandra Steele's emotional state are on full display. Puffy around the eyes, pink under the nose. She has been crying. The swelling doesn't hide the dark circles, she has not been sleeping. The fidgety hands, the discomposure; something has her on edge.

Sandra clears her throat, her words coming out gruff, as though she has not used her voice in some time. Or perhaps has overused it.

"I require a word with your son, Jacob."

A peremptory statement, not a request. Maureen is taken aback by her impertinence.

A silent exchange passes between husband and wife before she responds with equal brazenness.

"Be that as it may, I do not appreciate your tone, Ms. Steele. Nor do I feel particularly inclined to accommodate your request, if that is indeed what this is." Her nostrils flare.

The two women stand toe to toe, sizing up one the other. Peter interjects.

"Let's try this again, shall we? Ms. Steele, might we ask for a little context? You are clearly upset, and we would like to help."

The diplomacy has a definite effect. Maureen watches Sandra wilt like a desiccated flower, her bravado melting away. Inwardly she jeers at Peter for such an unwarranted display of empathy. *She* started it after all.

"Please forgive me, I am just not myself since—"

She trails off, her eyes going to the window looking into nothing but blue sky. All three agents stand in silence for an uncomfortable minute.

"Ms. Steele?" Peter tries again.

"Yes, well, I'm sure you both know by now what has befallen my daughter."

Maureen has flashbacks of the farmhouse, the tea, the antidote, the wolf. Draeger insisting she be eliminated. And at her own hand no less. But she didn't go through with it. She is uncharacteristically speechless.

"Oh, my heavens, Ms. Steele, we had no idea. I am truly sorry." Peter's voice shakes just a little as he delivers his condolence.

"I was going through her camera roll and noticed an inordinate number of photographs of Everett and your son. They must have been close. I found it odd that he did not even attend her funerary service."

Sandra looks confused, realizing that this is news to Maureen and her husband.

"I am surprised to be honest. Ms. Domanso, are you not the chief Biodome analyst now? The purveyor of correction statistics? Surely you would have logged my daughter's passing by now?"

Maureen's mind is churning so fast the room begins to spin. She retrieves her tablet from a bureau nestled into a nook in the dining room. Fingers fly over screen after screen with the ease of practice. The tapping stops, she scrolls down and then back up. Her gut clenches.

"The correction is not logged."

Sandra's eyes narrow.

"Whatever do you mean? Aren't all corrections logged in the Biodome archive?"

"Yes, yes they are," Maureen feels like she is standing on quicksand. Jacob is not logged either, yet he remains missing. This cannot be a coincidence; this has the stink of Draeger all over it.

"So, what are you saying?" Sandra and Peter both stare at her.

"It means your daughter did not succumb to a righting protocol. Yet she is gone. Just like Jacob."

Chapter 4

'Fracture for fracture, eye for an eye, tooth for a tooth, just as he had caused a disfigurement against another man, so it is to be done against him.'
—Leviticus 24:20 (ISV)

Draeger is roused by a light shake of his shoulder. It takes him a moment to recognize his surroundings as his brain slows to transition from the dream world.

"Tell me son, how do you feel? Your corporeal form has improved markedly."

Father steps back bringing his material perfection into full view.

Draeger blinks away the sleep and assesses. The pounding in his head has subsided while the searing heat along his spine has receded considerably. No longer sweating, no more tremors. A wave of relief ripples over him.

"Much better Father, thank you."

The patriarch looks pleased. He inclines his head to Chinda, his way of saying thanks. She beams. Sanstrom puffs out his chest and lifts his chin with self-importance. When Father does not acknowledge him, he inserts himself into the conversation.

"Yes well, you are welcome. I am only glad I could be of assistance. I will take my payment now," he licks his lips, lowers his head playfully and, raising only his eyes, holds a pornographic gaze on Chinda, "and be on my very merry way."

Draeger watches as the diminutive warrior flinches, recoiling from this filthy wretch of a man.

Father's contentment slips as a wall of angry storm clouds roll over his features.

"Tell me, doctor, how is it that you manage to be *persona non grata* even here, among the most wicked and depraved?"

Sanstrom is not deterred; singly focused on his prey, he tries another tact.

"A deal is a deal. At least, I thought you were a man of honor."

A dangerous challenge.

"You speak of honor as though it is somehow noble to defile, to dishonor your victims. Very well then, honorable Dr. Sanstrom. You may take Chinda as you please."

Draeger is astonished by Father's capitulation. Chinda is equally surprised, a look of hurt ghosting across her pretty face. Sanstrom is rubbing his hands together like he is about to enjoy a gourmet feast when Father speaks one last time.

"However, I am certain you found little satisfaction in preying on helpless females during your time on Earth. The sedation would have made for such easy fodder, the victories dull, hollow even. No, this time you will conquer your quarry like the honorable man you are. Chinda is yours, as promised. All you have to do is subdue the poor little helpless girl."

Chinda returns to Draeger's chamber one hour later wiping the blade of her *jian*. The razor-sharp double-edged sword is one of the many ancient weapons in her arsenal, her craft had demanded versatility. Now these deadly tools are her playthings.

Draeger is sitting up in the bed, propped up with several oversize, silk-covered pillows. He is feeling more robust and fit by the minute. He raises an eyebrow at her as she flicks a piece of pink fleshy matter into the fire. It sizzles. Draeger does not want to know.

"In the Lake of Fire," she says simply in response to his unasked question.

She muses while inspecting the blade in the orange glow, "Suffice it to say he won't be gawping, or molesting anything, ever again."

Father steps back into the bed chamber. He is wearing his official robe, the deepest midnight blue with a black, diamond-encrusted chain of office around his neck. His raven locks are loose, falling like gossamer silk around his face, accentuating his alabastrine skin and angular jawline.

He does not seem surprised by Chinda's reappearance. It was a brilliantly orchestrated maneuver; Father remained true to his word while his pet warrior was never really in any danger.

"If this is any indication," Father nods approvingly at his son, "a full recovery is imminent. Presently, I must attend to council matters. My impending departure necessitates the appointment of a proxy in my absence. Upon my return, we shall prepare you for your return to the Biodome. And mine to the Beginning."

Father regards Chinda.

"I trust you will assist in ambulating the prince."

She bows her head in deference.

"As you wish, my Lord."

With a flourish of his opulent robes, Draeger watches Father turn on his heel and exit the chamber. He would have liked another day or two to rest and recuperate but alas, the patriarch has spoken. He lifts the fur blanket from his lap and winces as he swings his legs over the edge of the bed. Chinda is at his side in an instant, supporting him by the elbow as he tries to bear his weight on shaky legs.

"Deep breaths," she advises. "This has been quite an ordeal, even for you."

Draeger steadies himself, the spots clearing from his vision. He inhales as instructed, feeling a constriction in his back, suddenly easing upon exhalation. Something rubs against his skin.

"Chinda, the mirror if you will."

She complies, dragging a massive full-length dressing mirror encased in a thick, black marble frame, to his bedside. The ancient bronze claw feet protest against the floor, yet she moves it as though it were a plastic replica and not an original furnishing courtesy of one condemned pharaoh. She was definitely never in any real danger from the filthy Dr. Sanstrom.

Draeger unknots the sash on his silk robe. It falls away, exposing a chiseled chest and perfectly sculpted abdomen, honeyed, unblemished skin pulled taught. He watches Chinda's reflection, her eyes roving up and down his torso admiringly.

Her expression changes from one of approbation to one of alarm when she shifts her focus to his backside. Draeger rotates his body slowly, looking over his shoulder, never taking his eyes off the mirror.

No Father, you are so wrong, a full recovery will never be. A sheet of molten skin, the scaley ridges protruding in a repeating pattern, sloughs off his back, sliding to the floor at his feet. In its place, the shiny red iridescence of a brand-new reptilian integument extends from his shoulder blades to the small of his back, a black-slitted iris at its center, like a bull's eye.

The crick in my neck can no longer be ignored. I have to straighten my spine or risk permanent disfigurement. As I shift my weight, Achilles stirs underneath me, perks his ears, and with a big sigh, decides he's not ready to get up.

I gently extricate myself and get to work on the kink, rubbing vigorously. It's dark, it takes a second for my eyes to adjust. The glow of the moon throws dim bolts of light through the vine curtains. I almost jump out of my skin when two glowing orbs hover in the air to my left. His eyes are open, watching me.

"Jake!" I scramble to my knees.

"Hello, stranger, fancy finding you here," his voice is thick, but there is strength in it.

"Jake," I repeat. "How do you feel? Does it hurt? What can I do?" I sound like a ninny, one question tripping over the next.

Jake exhales slowly, "That depends, I have no idea how I've come to be in this predicament in the first place."

He rolls onto his back, lifting the offended hand in the air.

"This smarts something awful though," He scrunches up his nose. "And what, pray tell, is that smell?"

I snicker at the look on his face.

"Yes, well, that's you actually."

He looks positively horrified.

"But it's much better than it was. It will be gone before long."

Achilles lifts his head. I think it's the first time Jake has noticed him.

"Whoa," his chin disappears into his neck as he tries to scoot backwards on the little pallet.

"It's okay, Jake, he's a friend. This is Achilles. I've sort of, acquired him, I guess you could say, or maybe it's the other way around. Sometimes, I'm not sure. Either way, he saved your life. I never would have known how to treat that," I gesture to the arm, "without him. Don't let those baby blues fool you, there's a genius in there. Isn't there boy?"

I ruffle the fur around his ears, much to his delight. The wolf leans into my hands.

Jake nods slowly. He is surrounded by magnificent creatures all day long; he probably assumes Achilles is just another great beast from the garden. I don't dispel the notion, which would take too much explaining. And besides, I'm still puzzled myself how the Waheela came to be my companion across dimensions.

"As to your first question, that despicable little four-legged reprobate seems to really have it out for you."

Now, he looks truly shocked. "What? Here? That's impossible, I got rid of him. This is the—"

He doesn't finish.

"The Beginning. I got that."

I think back to my math lesson with Evander not that long ago.

"Ground zero," I don't explain the reference, no time for that now.

"And we both know what happened the first time. But I don't think he's gonna be satisfied with temptation and a little red apple this time."

Jake tries to sit up. I push him back down gently.

"But Everett. What are you saying? This is a do-over?"

"Something like that, yes, I believe it is."

"But Evey," he is almost whispering now, "in the Beginning there were two."

I don't know when I realized it. I had my suspicions, a deep-seated feeling, an intuition I suppose. But I think it became real when I woke from sleep this morning and yet, I'm still here. In my mind's eye, I replay the last time I saw my family, my home.

I had snuck into Evander's room, watched him sleep, kissed him goodbye. The last thing I said was in the privacy of my bedroom, staring at the ceiling, thinking no one was listening. Even feeling a little foolish for speaking the words. But speak them I did. And I must have meant it.

Permission granted.

Wandering Tree is deceptively astute. With Tank hot on his heels, he breaks trail seemingly from memory, although he insists the tells of their journey from the outcropping are plain as day in the underbrush.

He points to a broken twig, a patch of matted green moss, the scuffed bark of a strangler fig. The extra-large team of man and beast have to pause every 30 feet or so while Pedro closes the gap, his much shorter legs taking two steps for every one of the giant's.

It is not lost on Pedro that this man carried his dead weight on his back on this very path only a few days ago. The man hasn't even broken a sweat. By comparison, Pedro's shortness of breath and the lactic acid accumulating in his thighs are subtle indications that he really ought to dedicate some personal time to cardiovascular exercise. For now, he'll blame it on his recent ordeal.

He realizes that it is going to take time for his body to adjust to the missing hand, but he is amazed that after only a few days of relying on the non-dominant left side, his dexterity is improving by leaps and bounds. But he still deems the upcoming journey necessary. If there is even a chance he can make himself whole again, he must return, reluctant as he might be.

The ancients perfected the prosthetic limb. Centuries of conflict after conflict, IEDs, landmines, and infected wounds provided a steady stream of soldiers suffering the same traumatic amputations as Pedro has. The ancients even had a compensation system in place, combatants paid for severed limbs, so long as said limbs were lost in the line of duty.

The cost of war they called it, as though ancient governments could buy back the lives of the foot soldiers who sacrificed themselves for their country. Pedro shudders at the thought, but there is a silver lining, thin as it may be. The Biodome just might have retained the technology that could build him a new hand.

A break in the monotony rouses Pedro from his musings. The temperature rises several degrees as Wandering Tree leads him out from under the cover of the forest canopy onto a cobbled pathway, the massive Ceará Plateau rising like a stone giant on the horizon. He forces in a deep breath to quell an uneasiness stirring in the pit of his stomach.

He reminds himself that he is not going beyond the jeep. He will never again set foot on that unholy ground. The thought does little to mollify his nervous tension. They walk the rest of the way in complete silence, Tank scouting ahead and doubling back, Wandering Tree perfectly in tune with the dog's cues, confident all is well. For his part, Pedro can't shake the feeling that this is a death march.

Chapter 5

'Not only so, but we also glory in our sufferings, because we know that suffering produces perseverance; perseverance, character; and character, hope.'

—Romans 5:3–4 (NIV)

Draeger shields his eyes from the glaring sun as he steps out of the cave. His ears pick up a distinct droning on either side of the entrance, the stench of the corpse flowers an aphrodisiac for the melee of itinerant flies. His normally lithe frame protests still, a most foreign sensation that reminds Draeger of the gravity of the affliction.

He is incensed by the boy's impudence but, grudgingly, respects his self-abnegation. His proclivity for reprisal is stifled; even if the boy lives, he cannot exact revenge, his proverbial hands are tied. He scoffs at his own childish supposition as it slips from his lips, unbidden.

"Dumb rule."

He moves slowly, feeling the limits of his wracked body, gently coaxing himself forward. Father's patience is exhausted, the time for weakness is over. By the time he emerges from the twisted foliage of the hellscape, his muscles, having yielded to the stimulation, regain some modicum of vigor. The worst of it now behind him, his mood lightens along with his step.

The black spot in his field of vision gradually morphs into the large overland vehicle he drove here days ago, stationed exactly where he parked it.

He catches a scent in the air, corroborated by the kettle of vultures circling intently above. But not just blood, human blood. The corners of his mouth curve into a barbed grin. Perhaps the boy was subject to divine retribution after all.

Draeger surmises the boy must have returned at some point. The tailgate swings on its hinges, as if the jeep were abandoned in a hurry. He glances upward, the buzzards are centered directly above the truck. Yes, an inducement is very near.

He is startled by an enormous dog that bounds out of nowhere. The animal lopes in his direction on powerful legs, tongue dangling from a slobbery mouth, smooth white canine teeth on full display.

Now where did this beast come from? he wonders.

He hears a shrill whistle that stops the dog dead in its tracks. It turns tail and doubles back. There. A giant head bobs up over a knoll. This one he does not recognize, but the second, much smaller figure that emerges over the hillock, challenges his self-control. Heat waves rise from his uncollared shirt, rippling the air around his face. The dog makes a second appearance, this time heeled at the larger human's side.

So, if young Pedro lives, then who is the owner of the coppery tang coming from the jeep? There is no mistake, it is the blood of man. Confused, he pokes his head into the front of the vehicle. He checks the front bumper, then the tires. Nothing. Finally, he skirts the open tailgate and peers into the back of the jeep.

Draeger looks back to Pedro, watching the boy as he scrambles up the incline. That is all the confirmation he needs. He was not mistaken; it was the boy's blood. But it is not the boy, but the remnants of his right forelimb. Maggots feast on the rotten meat hanging off the carpals and metacarpals, the phalanges picked clean. A blood-soaked axe lay discarded beside the grisly mess.

Nothing divine here, this is nothing more than self-mutilation. Draeger flashes back to the last few days. The pain, the delirium, the certainty that his human half would not, could not, survive. It appears young Pedro came to the same conclusion.

He heaves a sigh.

"Clever boy."

He chooses a more surreptitious entry this time. One of the small advantages of this hideous form. No need for deadly venom today. Or bone-crushing strength. He will have need of his cottonmouth and copperhead and constrictor in due time. No, today, He requires a more obscure skill afforded his caste. Hovering at the precipice of the nexus, He slithers away from the cave entrance, deeper into darkness.

The walls close in with each propulsion of his sinewy body until it is little more than a crevice that no bipedal species could navigate. Using his hypersensitive olfactory and vomeronasal systems together, He works his forked tongue in and out, in and out, searching. Finally, his patience is rewarded.

He reaches deep within his vast genetic repertoire, calling on his *Hydrophiinae* lineage and assumes the characteristics of the sea krait for the long journey ahead. He dives headfirst into the aquifer and descends until He finds the underground artery that leads to the Beginning. And then He swims.

It's been almost seven hours since He last surfaced for air, testing the limits of his oversize lung. Thanks to this body's unique design, oxygen continues to permeate his skin membrane but the specialized vascular network on his head and snout are struggling to capture enough of the vital element to sustain brain function. The mild hypoxia is dizzying, black spots floating in and out of focus.

He calculates; it must be close. He picks up the pace, his body becoming one with the water, up anticlines and down synclines of a folded mountain range, then speeding along a flat expanse like a bullet train. The rollercoaster waterway makes its final ascent, climbing the steep incline of a majestic dome mountain. He eyes the discharge point up ahead. Just a little farther.

He breaks through the water spring about halfway up the mountain, gulping in air like a half-starved king crocodile, electrifying his starved neurons. He scans his new surroundings. Well above the tree line, the mountainside is spotted with stunted shrubbery; stone pine, mountain heather, tiny purple and white bell flowers clinging precariously to spindly stems.

Only the hardiest alpine vegetation can survive the harsh climate extremes and even harsher soil conditions at this altitude. A light tan-colored pika, half-rabbit, half-mouse, scuttles in the scree below the spring, two yellow-bellied marmots not far behind, seeking refuge.

Even the basest of creatures are wise to the danger of his arrival. As He watches the trio disappear from sight, He quips to himself. Almost comical how the obtuse human could learn a thing or two from a simple rodent.

Pedro sits in a sparsely furnished corner office off the main hall. The Department of Health Promotion occupies this relic of a building, known as a hospital in ancient times. Drab grey rubber tiled floors, faded and scuffed beige paint, harsh fluorescent lighting recessed into decrepit, water-stained ceiling tiles, some rooms made up of nothing more than blue-green curtains.

There were over 100,000 such facilities throughout the Biodome at the time of the Correction with territorial governments pouring trillions into the health care machine. And yet, a chronic deficit in beds and services plagued a civilization that treated their minds and bodies with such flagrant disregard. They convinced themselves that they were somehow entitled to unlimited care for their follies.

Even worse, those same governments often created the health crises themselves; a proliferate drug, alcohol, and tobacco supply, a proliferate weapon supply, a proliferate war machine, economic agendas that guaranteed a steady supply of impoverished families, impoverished communities, impoverished countries. Governments playing God with secret lab experiments, manipulating virulent pathogens only to feign ignorance when it all went to hell in a handbasket.

As he awaits the agent from health promotion and the second one from engineering assisting in his care, Pedro sits on the edge of the thin mattress, rubbing the small of his back. His plan to drive the jeep back into the city was scuppered rather abruptly when he crested that last ridge.

There he was, leaning against the front of the jeep, arms crossed, the ghost of a smirk on his perfect lips, toeing a large stone like a soccer ball, like he didn't have a care in the world. Like his spine was never torn asunder. Like he was never infected with the deadliest poison known to man.

They had locked eyes, a silent exchange. The words of the old medicine man came back with haunting clarity in that moment. *You cannot kill the one who is already dead.*

The retreat was torture, Wandering Tree had to fashion a slip collar from a Liana vine to restrain Tank who wanted nothing more than to confront Dr. Draeger. Bad. Idea.

Wandering Tree was not immune to the malevolence in the air as he spoke to the dog in his native tongue, "Não não menino. Existe o mal lá."

Pedro had interpreted in his head. *Yes boy, he is right, there is evil here.*

They had slumped down in front of the fire, even Wandering Tree seemed worse for the wear after the arduous trek there and back. Pedro felt the edges of his consciousness give way until Morning Sun approached from the riverbank, water glistening off her rich black hair, her face even more striking without the war paint.

Tired as he was, Pedro thought she might have been a hallucination, but he straightened up and shook the cobwebs from his brain, just in case. She had raised an eyebrow at him as she looked him up and down.

"Could not resist our hospitality *Mão Roubada?*" she teased.

Very real. He swallowed, it felt like sand was mixed in with saliva. Wandering Tree raised his eyes. Supported by elbows, he was bowed forward, his head between his knees. He looked at each of them in turn, barked a little half grunt, half laugh and returned his eyes to the ground.

From out of nowhere, a surly voice had called out in alarm.

"*Sol da Manhã! Voltam.* Back away!"

Everyone went very still. Tank lay flat against the ground, a soft whimper carried away by the wind. Morning Sun was the first move, treading backwards as she was bade. Grandfather only used that tone when he was deadly serious. Walks in the Rain hobbled into the circle of the fire pit and turned to Wandering Tree and Pedro.

"You three," he looked at the dog, "both man and animal, you smell of death and decay. Your spirits, they weep. They suffer."

That night, Walks in the Rain performed a smudging ceremony, burning a generous amount of the sacred medicines. The potent mixture of tobacco, cedar, sage, and sweetgrass had clung to Pedro's lungs.

Wandering Tree and even Tank had been solemn as the old medicine man performed the ritual. Pedro was so relieved when Walks in the Rain announced that their souls were freed from the dark shadows, he let out a long breath he didn't know he had been holding.

A little while later, he sat by the riverbank with Morning Sun, the moonlight dancing off the gently flowing water. She had asked him to stay. Part of him, a large part of him, wanted to say yes.

The next morning, he sat on the back of a horse, a strong-willed dapple-grey stallion named *Lua Cheia,* Full Moon. The muscled animal sensed his weariness, he had never been on horseback before. Full Moon took full advantage of his timid rider, toying with him. Pulling the reins from Pedro's hands, tossing his head like a crazed fool, picking up a quick trot without prompting, sending Pedro bouncing, jarring his spine with each footfall, dangerously close to capsizing him. Wandering Tree threw his head back and laughed, regaled with Pedro's ineptness.

The giant's horse, a brown and white painted Gypsy Vanner, big enough to carry his massive frame comfortably, never once stepped out of line. He'd later blamed it all on his one-handedness, but truth be told, 10 hands wouldn't have saved him the embarrassment of his maiden voyage on horseback.

Wandering Tree left him at the research outpost, the locals had stared from the cover of their overhangs as they passed through the village. The building was secluded, he had to dispatch agents to retrieve him. The same look of shock crossed everyone's features when they saw him. He had concocted a reasonable explanation.

He had suffered a terrible accident while he trekked through the rainforest that had cost him his hand. Pedro has rehearsed his lines, alluding to a run-in with a black caiman while paddling through the shallows of a stream deep in the basin. Agents were too polite to press for details, oozing sympathy for Pedro. His mother had cried, but his father remained stoic.

Back in the present, he brings his fingers to his lips, remembering Morning Sun's chaste kiss right before she left him sitting at the river's edge.

Her last words to him, "In case you change your mind."

When the agents appear in the doorway, the daydream, and the girl's beautiful face, melt away, leaving Pedro feeling a little forlorn. To his relief, the agents are all business, they don't even seem to notice his dismay.

He perks up when the engineering agent places a black hardcover case on the bed, a broad smile spreading across his face. A proud smile, almost identical to the one the health promotion agent is flashing. Her enthusiasm bleeds through her pronouncement.

"Mr. Ramón, I come bearing gifts," she giggles. "I believe Mr. Belvedeere here and I have outdone ourselves."

She gives a self-satisfied nod to her colleague. Mr. Belvedeere pops the fasteners on the case and flourishes his hand as he lifts the lid like a magician putting on a child's show. Pedro's eyes go wide when he sees his hand, a perfect replica actually, resting in a foam mold in the case.

The prosthetic limb is so accurate, it even has the palmar flexion creases to match his left hand, the olive skin tone, and the texture, it looks so real no one would know the difference. Except him. Except for the stub of titanium protruding from the wrist end of the prosthesis.

"May I?" asks the engineering agent.

Dr. Crenshaw looks on expectantly, urging him with her eyes.

"Ugh, *si*, yes, I guess."

He feels squeamish when the lifeless latex touches the stump for the first time, his stomach somersaulting. The agent proceeds carefully, explaining as he works, reassuring him that his reaction is completely normal. Dr. Crenshaw nods, patting his shoulder.

"You're doing great Pedro. The brain is an incredible organ, you will adjust. In no time, you will accept the prosthesis without thinking twice."

After the final fitment and minor adjustments, the device is vacuum sealed to his arm with suction sockets. It fits like a glove.

Dr. Draeger undertakes his first order of business to re-establish the chain of command now that he has returned to the Biodome. His lieutenant waits on the other side of the door; he is making her wait an unnecessary moment longer, just to make his point.

She may have become a tad too comfortable in the driver's seat in his absence. She can stew all she wants; the little bird must be put back into her cage. Another three minutes pass before he admits her. He walks to the door on silent soles and opens the door.

"Ms. Domanso," is all he says.

He is mildly disappointed, noting she does not look irritated or flummoxed in the least. In fact, she looks radiant in a tailored pantsuit in dusty rose, a vanilla-tinted librarian blouse and matching six-inch heels completing the look. Her chin held high, her eyes bright and overflowing with self-confidence, she is the embodiment of grace. She has adjusted rather well it seems.

"Welcome back, Sir," she offers upon entering the office. "No doubt you will want to be updated. I have compiled performance data for all departments in all quadrants for the last two weeks."

She produces the report from her handbag, placing it on the edge of his desk.

Right down to business. She has not skipped a beat.

"And what of our esteemed cabinet members? I trust they have been compliant in my absence. There is that ancient maxim after all, when the cat's away, the mice will play."

"Oh no, Sir. There has been no misbehavior, no dereliction of duty whatsoever. The cabinet has been executing exactly as instructed."

As Draeger absorbs the news, it becomes anticlimactic. He was so certain his presence was quintessential to maintaining the subterfuge. That these lowly humans could not possibly pull off a deception of this magnitude without his grandeur. He cannot very well admonish the woman. For what? For being too competent, too adroit?

"I see," he utters, throwing the cover of the report open and glancing at the graphs and figures.

"Sir, we are right on track to meet your targets. I am personally overseeing all labor and production reporting. No need to bore yourself with minor details, it's all right here for you."

Draeger scrutinizes his assistant. Something is not quite right but he can't put his finger on it. It's all just a little too perfect. Mr. Ashton was an unsophisticated liar, his misrepresentations easily discernible. Perhaps it is time to delve a little deeper.

He reaches across the desk. Just as he is about to grasp her hand, a desperate rap at his office door causes him to abandon the assault. The door flies open and a sweaty agent, one of his very own cabinet members, comes flying across the threshold.

"Henry, my goodness, what is it?" Maureen appears genuinely puzzled.

"Ms. Domanso, come, quickly. There has been a breach in the northeast quadrant. The natives are refusing to surrender their grain quota for the month."

The young agent seems to catch himself.

"Wait," he bows slightly. "Now that Dr. Draeger has returned, Sir, could you not simply—"

Draeger stares straight ahead, stone-faced, his brain scrambling to formulate a plausible excuse. It is taking more time than he likes. He is saved by his assistant.

"Oh Henry, Dr. Draeger does not have time for this tomfoolery. There is really no need to invoke the existential virus."

She looks to Dr. Draeger for confirmation.

"Sir, if you will excuse me, I will attend to this trivial matter on your behalf. As I said, I am here to insulate you from the absurdities of the masses. Not to worry, I am most effective in keeping everyone in check. This is nothing more than a hiccup."

She does not take leave without permission, standing at the ready, like a trained dog.

"Indeed, Ms. Domanso," he looks at Henry to emphasize his next point. "As you said, I have much more pressing affairs of state to attend. You are excused."

With a dutiful curtsy, Maureen follows Henry out the door, leaving Draeger wondering as the hurried click of her heels fades down the hall.

He breathes a little sigh of relief. Perhaps she is just that good. Perhaps he chose *too* well.

Chapter 6

'The mob believes everything it is told, provided only that it be repeated over and over. Provided too that its passions, hatreds, fears are catered to. Nor need one try to stay within the limits of plausibility: on the contrary, the grosser, the bigger, the cruder the lie, the more readily is it believed and followed.'
—Alexandre Koyré, Réflexions sur le mensonge (1945)

Maureen stands at the window of the derelict abattoir on the outskirts of this midwestern backward farming town, waiting for her retinue. Flies congeal on the old '*S*' hooks where carcasses once hung in row upon row upon row. She wrinkles her nose at the swarming insects attracted by the decades-old smell of slaughter.

Gary, from the Department of Agriculture, suggested this location, away from prying eyes, and more importantly, Dr. Draeger. A resistance movement always needs an underground lair. Not exactly underground *per se*, but Maureen is certain they will evade suspicion hidden behind the walls of this filthy abandoned stockyard.

Henry was brilliant earlier today, such dramatic flair. Even Domanso would have believed the crisis to be real had she not orchestrated the facade herself. She is more convinced now than ever that Draeger no longer has command of the virus. He failed her little test, the blank look on his face said it all.

She also worried that he might become dubious; he needed to see her in action to appreciate her value as his First Minister, to remind him that she considers his hands far too noble to be soiled by mundane squabbles.

Leave it to the little soldiers in the trenches to do the dirty work. It's all part of the plan. Draeger's inattention is a prerequisite to his derogation and eventual dethroning.

Gary is the first to arrive, seemingly immune to the ghastly surroundings. Much to Maureen's dismay, he pulls up an ancient three-legged stool, red streaks soaked into the grain of the wood, and plops himself down, letting out a puff of air.

"So, what do you think? Pretty cool right? As far as secret meeting places go."

She pulls a sanitizing wipe from her bag and begins rubbing vigorously at her hands, lifting the cuticles on her fingernails in her zeal. She reaches for another wipe.

"Out of necessity, I would agree. It will serve."

She walks to a grimy window, stopping short of wiping the pane. The distinct sound of tires on gravel announces the next arrival. They start pouring in one after the other. Six agents come in pairs, but most have travelled alone. Maureen insists all cars be parked in the back, out of view.

It makes for an oxymoronic sight; twelve shiny, sleek sedans, identical but for coloring, lined up with military precision along the dented old metal siding speckled with mud and manure and rust spots. Safe to say, Draeger will never look here.

With the exception of Gary, everyone stands, clustered in an invisible bubble, away from the walls, avoiding contact with any and all surfaces. Maureen glares at the holdout and finally, Gary joins the huddle.

"Yes, well, I admit, this is certainly not the type of meeting accommodations we are accustomed to, but discretion is of utmost importance."

Gary rolls his eyes. Maureen clenches her teeth at the gesture but chooses diplomacy instead.

"Therefore, I think we owe Gary a debt of gratitude."

Message sent. And received. Everyone nods in turn to the DOA agent. By all accounts, he is appeased by the acknowledgement. Maureen is keenly aware that a ruffled feather could be the bare thread that unravels this nervous alliance. Once she is certain Gary's ego has been satiated, she takes a deep breath.

"Despite the indigence of our surroundings, there is a certain fitness about us that I find indisputable. Tell me, are there any among us who have suffered a righting protocol since we've abandoned the blue box?"

Edith, an older agent handpicked by Draeger in his original draft, stands up taller and addresses the group.

"I personally, have never felt better. I seem to have made a miraculous recovery since we began this little crusade of ours."

Agreement all the way around. Maureen smiles.

"So, you see, we must be on the side of righteousness. The Biodome is sending us a message. Dr. Draeger must be stopped. And we are tasked with stopping him."

Gary vocalizes what Maureen is certain they are all thinking.

"Yes, but we can only undermine his orders for so long, how long can we fudge the reports before he figures it out? All it will take is one site inspection and he will be on to us."

"You are not wrong," Maureen agrees. "First let me confirm the truth of the matter. He is indeed returned. From where I do not know. I dared not ask."

She looks at Henry and nods approvingly. "At great risk to himself, Henry helped me convince Dr. Draeger that all is well in the Biodome, exactly as he left it. He is none the wiser of our deception. As Gary has pointed out, for the moment."

"So, we are at a stalemate then, we have no move!" Gary is clearly frustrated.

Maureen is not deterred.

"I think not. You see, it is all an illusion. A great lie. Dr. Draeger does not control the existential virus. Not anymore. I am certain of it."

The group look at one another, doubt furrowed in drawn brows, uncertainty in the slight turn and retreat of heads, as though they are pulling away from a flame. Another of the original cabinet is the first to speak up.

"Ugh, have you forgotten what he did to Heather Charlemagne? To Nesbitt and Merkel?"

Maureen interrupts him.

"Of course I have not forgotten! But no longer. He has lost command of the virus. All we have to do is expose the lie, publicly. He will be denounced, his reign of terror over. Harmony, integrity, purpose, purpose of our own choosing, returned to the Biodome."

Young agent 2944, the group's budding historian, offers his thoughts. Maureen hardly recognizes him since she last saw him. He is clean-cut, clean-shaven, shoulders proud and square, his eyes beaming with intellect and potential.

"They all fall down."

He pauses, everyone stares. He clears his throat.

"Resistance is a common theme throughout human history. It goes by many names; insurgency, the independence movement, civil uprising, coup d'état. Anti-fascism, anti-communism, anti-Nazism." He waits, reassured by the silence that they are listening, and then continues.

"The records are replete with example after example of resistance where the abuses of power became intolerable, even in so-called democratic societies. All resistance movements had one thing in common. They sought to dispel the myth created by the oppressors. To expose the lie that enabled the oppression. Ms. Domanso is right."

If he's talking to himself or to the group, Maureen is unsure, but either way, she is indebted to him for the rousing testimony. Now they all start talking at once. Oddly, it is Edith who rises above the crescendo, striking a rusted metal table with a length of alloy steel chain hanging from the ceiling. The clang of metal on metal makes Maureen jump. Edith lifts her chin like a schoolteacher scolding her students.

"Now then, assuming agent Domanso is correct, the question becomes how to expose Dr. Draeger for the liar he is."

Maureen picks up the mantle.

"I have a plan. I will denigrate one of us publicly for a transgression so contemptible Dr. Draeger will have no choice but to invoke the existential virus. When he fails to wield his weapon, the truth will be revealed, he has no deterrent. The illusion will be exposed."

Gary pouts his lips.

"And if you are wrong?"

The question hangs in the air. There is no need to answer, everyone knows what will happen if she is wrong.

"I am not wrong," she reiterates with absolute conviction.

After a determined pause, she buries the irritation in her voice and changes tact, choosing a more mollifying tone.

"Now then, we simply need a volunteer to commit the unthinkable. Who will stand before the Biodome and publicly reject Dr. Draeger?"

Silence.

They all stand looking at one another, suddenly mute, each and every one of them.

"Why don't you do it?" Gary sputters.

Maureen faces Gary.

"I must maintain the ruse. I am too close to him; he watches my movements closely. I am at his beck and call; he will know something is amiss. There is too much, intimacy, between us."

She is frustrated with having to explain what should be obvious.

"I am already doing double duty, acting as his trusted advisor while plotting his overthrow. I will do it if I must, but I fear I will not get far before he discovers my duplicity."

Still, no one speaks. Maureen sighs.

"Very well."

An unseen voice emanates from the far end of the abattoir. All heads swivel in the direction of the disembodied pledge.

"I'll do it."

Like an apparition, Sandra Steele emerges from the shadows.

Jake is up and about; his idea of convalescence includes fetching water and playing fetch with Achilles. Not surprisingly, he has bonded with the great wolf, they are becoming fast friends. I think he is filling a void inside Jake, remnants of the loss of his beloved dog. Achilles seems only too happy to play the pet.

I know he is not here to be our plaything; I have seen firsthand that this creature is far more astute than any ordinary companion animal. But it is heartwarming to watch Jake's face light up when they are together. He's been through so much; I don't have it in me to redirect his attention to the very real threat of *operation tetra*.

And besides, my hypervigilance is enough for both of us. My head feels like it's on a swivel, 24/7. I look everywhere, all the time. In the tree, under rocks, in tall grass, anywhere the beast could be hiding, lying in wait to hurt Jake again. Not on my watch.

I am coming to terms with my choice. The arrow is still lodged deep in my heart. I feel it most when I think of my family, what they must have endured, how they must have suffered at my passing. The unanswered questions they must have. I reach for memories, resolute in keeping them from fading. It's all

I have now. The weight on my conscience is overwhelming when I think of Mom, how I swept the rug right out from under her. I don't think I ever truly appreciated how my actions and choices would affect the people I love. It feels so selfish.

But then, I look at Jake. I watch his chest heave with each new breath, see the life coming back into his eyes, and the shame and guilt of what I have done to my family is tolerable.

"Where are you, Evey?" Jake is staring down at me.

I don't even know how long I've been sitting on this rock like a clam baking in the sun. His mouth turns downward in an exaggerated frown. I almost envy him, he doesn't appear to be grappling with his decision at all, he has never expressed any regrets. Maybe I just need more time.

"Jake, does it ever bother you, how you left your family behind?"

He considers a long minute before speaking.

"Ah, now I know what's got you all coiled up inside."

He sits down beside me and places his good arm around my shoulder, pulling me in. I'm not sure he is going to answer my question, but then he sighs.

"It's different for me Evey. If anything, I worry about my dad, he was always the nurturing one, at least in the last 10 years or so. My mom stopped caring when she was promoted to Senior Health Agent. I was 11. She stopped coming to my soccer games, stopped helping me with homework, heck Evey, she stopped making eye contact."

"I became a burden. She did give me Hercules, but I think that was more to distract me, so she didn't have to pay attention. The only thing that mattered to her was that I rise to her expectations as an agent of the Biodome. I'll bet she was relieved when I disappeared, saved her the embarrassment of admitting that she had a son who chose dogs."

He strokes Achilles' head.

"And apparently, wolves," I tease, trying to lighten the moment. I misjudged; I shouldn't have asked. There is a gaping wound there.

"I'm so sorry Jake," I don't know what else to say.

Now he strokes the top of my head as I lean against his chest.

"I traded my family for the Biodome. You traded yours for, me. I am the one who is sorry."

I sit up straight, and look him in the eye.

"Jacob Domanso, let's get one thing clear. Yes, I miss my family, yes, I might be struggling a little with the whole *never go back* thing, but I do not, not for one minute, regret choosing this. Choosing you."

He cups my chin, tilts my head up, and kisses me softly.

"I don't deserve you," he says. "There is no one else I would rather be stranded with in this garden."

Achilles lists his head sideways, blue eyes wide and pleading. There it is again, that uncanny intelligence. He knows he's just been slighted.

"And don't forget our boy here." I ruffle his burly chest.

We abandon the heavy talk and walk hand-in-hand toward the stream. I resist the urge to coddle him, Jake is determined to put the whole near-death thing in the rearview mirror. As we approach the stream, he picks up a heavy stick discarded from a nearby willow tree and lobs it into the water.

We both laugh as Achilles takes off at breakneck speed, bounding with a nimbleness incompatible with his bulky frame. We watch in anticipation of the big dive, but it doesn't come. Instead, the wolf reins himself in at the water's edge, flattens his ears, and lowers himself against the ground.

We can hear his throaty growl; it slows our approach. I am instantly back into reconnaissance mode; Achilles has articulated the imminent danger quite clearly.

I cannot find it. Where is that cursed thing? I follow the wolf's line of sight. He is looking directly at the water. I take Jake's hand as we reach the bank of the stream. There is no beast, but there is definitely peril on the horizon. The stream is undulating; tiny ripples wash over the water's surface, quivering with energy.

I watch the stick float downstream, swaddled in vibrations. My ears filter out sound, my vision processing everything in slow motion as the earth beneath my feet buckles and the sky turns black.

He makes his way up the side of the mountain, continuing to survey the landscape. The mountain dominates the eastern horizon, gently sloping on either side. Of course, it is a resplendent panorama, his nemesis has always been the ostentatious one. Why must He be so showy, so flamboyant. Victoria

Falls, the Great Barrier Reef, the Northern Lights, this picturesque garden. At least *He* can claim to be the sensible one. Hell is just, Hell. Fire and brimstone and more fire.

An idea begins to form in his mind. He may not have killed the boy, but surely he ails. His incapacitation is all but a certainty. The elixir He delivered, albeit only a dribble, was still lethal. Why, he will be ambulating in his abode this very minute, unable to defend himself with any degree of alacrity. Perhaps this is the perfect opportunity to borrow an adage from the ancients: *Kill two birds with one stone.*

Destroy the boy, yes, but also, why not obliterate the entire garden so there can be no more second chances? It is true that the Other controls earth, water, and air, but there is one element that remains firmly within *His* control. And it is anything but inconsequential. But fire will do him no good here, the Other will simply make rain.

No, He will have to be more creative. Yes indeed. The perfect place to set a new plan into action is underfoot. This mountain is a dome mountain. The little mountain that could. Magma rose from the mantle and pushed into the crust, but did not quite reach the surface. Well, maybe He can fix that.

He calls on his one element and it responds with ferocity, like the lion released from its cage. The fire swells in his veins, threatening to overtake his senses. He projects the flames into the core of the mountain. Like a Bunsen burner, He concentrates the heat under the apex and soon the igneous rock begins to transform, losing its shape as it reclaims its liquid properties.

It bubbles, the pressure building. Scree scatters down the mountainside, as though being swept away by an invisible hand. He intensifies the flame; the tremors respond in kind.

The eruption is presaged by an unearthly billowing black plume shooting high into the air like an ancient atomic bomb, blocking out the sunlight. And then, all hell breaks loose and the lava begins its descent.

Chapter 7

'The noise of battle is in the land and great destruction!'
—Jeremiah 50:22 (ESV)

Jake doubles over, cupping his arms over his head as the shockwave tests the limits of what his eardrums can withstand. He reaches for Everett as a blast of air pressure shoves her to the ground, her knees bearing the brunt of the fall, striking the sharp stones at the stream's edge.

He winces at the sight of blood blooming onto the hem of her shift. He comes to her side, squatting low and covering her as the sonic assault tears at their tympanic membranes.

He feels the rupture in his left ear as a sharp pain, his inner ear now exposed. He can feel the trickle of fluid leaking onto his earlobe and dripping onto his neck.

Achilles crawls on his belly toward them. Jake makes room for him in their embrace. There they cower, the three of them together, no match for this blitzkrieg.

Volcanic ash falls like snow, the pyroclastic fallout settling onto the surface of the water, on Achille's white coat, on Everett's tear-stained eyelashes. Jake feels an intense burning in his throat, his lungs being seared by the volcanic gases.

His eyes water in a desperate attempt to protect them. He tears at his tunic, ripping a sleeve into two long strips. His ears are ringing so badly, he can't find his voice, but he gently places a strip over Everett's nose and mouth and puts the other one over his own. The wolf will have to endure it.

Everett's eyes are wild. Fear is a rare look for this girl, but it is fear he sees now. Her eyes are rimmed in red, her sclera filled with broken blood vessels. Blood seeps from her nose and ears, the pressure of the blast is taking its toll on her.

The roar of the eruption finally subsides, the three sit in a puddle on the ground, watching in stunned silence as the glowing magma breaks from the crust of the summit and courses down the mountain like a dam that has suddenly burst.

He surveys his handiwork as it ravages the mountainside, the super-heated ultramafic lava, thick as molasses, wiping out everything in its deadly path. Trees burst into flame as the lava advances, surrendering to their maker. He relishes in the sight of it all. Looking upward, there is no end to the pyroclastic flow, it boils over in a steady torrent.

He runs ahead of the *pahoehoe* as it billows down the mountain and into the foothills, beckoning it onward. He slithers and stops, looking behind him at regular intervals, more elated with each scorching mile. For him, the heat is of no consequence, even in his current form.

Like an artist with a heavy stroke, all color is brushed away, replaced with monotonous charcoal black behind an advancing line of the boldest red. Just a little farther now, the goal within sight. He gauges, and surmises. He will reach his target. The encroaching lava begins to slow, the effusion from the mouth of the volcano finally out of fuel. No matter, it is enough. His computation is inerrant.

It stands tall and proud, refusing to combust, refusing to submit. Like his serpentiform brethren on a fat mouse, the lava swallows the Tree of Life whole. Finally sated, it comes to a halt.

He looks skyward through the fog of destruction, his eyes smiling.

Bet you didn't see that one coming.

I have a headache to end all headaches. I cannot escape the rhythmic throbbing, like the beating of powerful wings inside my brain. The nausea in my stomach roils with each pulse. The stream is only twenty feet across and shallow, barely coming up just past my waist, but I feel like I just swam the English Channel.

Jake and Achilles don't look much better. I don't think there is an ounce of energy left between the three of us. At least the water separates us from the devastation.

The land belches with black smoke as the fiery flow settles down the mountain, over the foothills and into the garden. Giant pillows of prehistoric komatiite, archaic igneous rock from the Precambrian period, settle over the landscape. Combined with a decidedly viridescent hue, the peculiar spinifex texture of the rock as it cools, it turns the countryside into an enigmatic mosaic.

I turn to face Jake. He is talking to me, gesticulating animatedly at the same time, like a mime. His ears must be ringing as mine do. He can't hear either. I take his hands to slow him down, nodding.

"Oh Kay," I mouth, "I am okay."

I point to my ears and shake my head. He nods in understanding.

I crouch before Achilles, wait until I am sure he has not gone feral from the stress of the situation, and reach out to pet him, looking for signs of injury. Red tinges his front paw, I gingerly pick it up and inspect. There is a deep laceration on the metacarpal pad, it is split almost into two pieces, like a broken heart.

The angry wound is caked with mud from our water crossing. Jake kneels beside me. Without speaking, we get to work. Jake soothes the wolf with reassuring strokes over his neck and face. I am still holding the strip of cloth Jake placed over my mouth. I wash it in the stream, black grit floats on the water's surface like oil. I soak it again and squeeze it over the paw. Jake hands me his clothes and I repeat.

It takes several trips to the stream and back to flush out the pad. Once it is reasonably clean, I lay the strips over one another and begin to wrap the foot, to protect it from infection. Jake puts his hand on mine to stop me.

"Neem," he half mouths, half speaks.

I must look puzzled because he adds another word to the message.

"Antiseptic," I just make out the word through the tinny ringing in my ears.

Achilles looks back and forth between us, the perfect patient. Jake disappears into the forest, returning minutes later with a fern-like stem and sprigs of green and yellow berries. He squeezes and mashes the vegetation into a pulpy material and then butters it over the strips of cloth.

Achilles watches me as I gently take the paw in my hand, his trust implicit as he allows me to tend to his injury. As I work, I chide myself for my ignorance. Between Achilles and his knowledge of anti-venoms and now Jake and his anti-infectants, I make a mental note to brush up on my botany.

We wash the worst of the grime off in the stream. I can still feel the grit in my mouth and chafing at my eyes every time I blink. I dunk my head and swirl my hair around, Jake mimics me while Achilles lies on the bank, overseeing our ministrations.

My heart drops when I look back across the stream at the carnage, a gaping hole in the landscape where our tree used to be the focal point of the garden.

"No point crossing back," I reason out loud, my words outstretched and slow. "It's probably safer to stay over here."

Jake nods but says nothing. He made the tree his home, our home. I think he is struggling with the gravity of our situation. I have to reassure him. I face him, take his hands in mine, look up into his solemn face.

The sun is just beginning to reappear behind me, rays streaming through the clouds and landing on his face, glistening off the water droplets falling from his curls, tiny crystals of light reflecting off his wet eyelashes. He has never looked more angelic than right now. I can hear my own voice now, muffled, but mercifully audible.

"Jake, we're going to be okay. We will survive, as long as we have each other."

He reaches for my face and wipes away pinkish water trickling down my jawline.

"Does it hurt?" he asks, as he reaches for his own earlobe. "It looks like you've lost both eardrums; I still have one intact. I think."

"Dizzy mostly," I say looking around, confirming the symptom as the land dips and sways.

I downplay the sharp pain that comes and goes, a random stabbing sensation that I can only hope will diminish over time.

"Same," he confesses.

Now he looks at the hem of my shift, spotted with blood from my fall.

"Just a little scrape," I brush away his concern.

I turn to practical matters to redirect his attention, raising my arms in the air.

"Well, it looks like we'll be dining under the stars tonight."

Jake's face twists as he glances across the stream.

"No, absolutely not. We will not dwell on what is done Jake."

I feel he is circling the drain and in real danger of being swept under. I cannot, will not, allow him to abandon hope.

"Now enough dallying, we've work to do."

Jake raises an eyebrow at my sassy tone, his lip curving into an impish grin.

"Lead the way, Miss Steele."

We fish the stream for Achilles who hobbles along on three paws. Hunting will be difficult in the coming days for him. Jake starts a small fire with two pieces of wood as easily as striking a match, smoke swirling from the sticks as he rubs them furiously against one another. The bounty is plentiful on this side of the waterway.

We gorge on mushrooms, sweet berries and cassava wrapped in wet palm leaves and softened over the fire. We cook the assortment of shiners and chub we collected from the creek and present them to Achilles. After a sniff or two, he devours the offering, little strings of saliva dangling from his lips.

I think he is content to stay off his feet for the moment, he sighs and flops his big head down against my leg. When he looks up at me, I can see the ash and smoke have taken a toll on him too, his sclera reddened behind the blue, much like my own I suspect.

Jake stifles a yawn, but it does little to hide his exhaustion. His limbs are heavy, his movements leaden. I gently extricate myself from Achilles and rise to help him. He groans softly as we gather leaf litter of prized palm leaves, layering them underneath the canopy of a healthy mahogany tree, the boughs stretching wide, weighed down with new growth. At least we will have some semblance of protection for the coming night. He makes to scavenge for more bedding, I block his path and take his wrists in my hands.

"It's enough, Jake. You need rest," I can hear myself more clearly now.

This sparks a little optimism; my hearing loss might just be temporary.

He does not protest. His shoulders slump and we walk hand-in-hand back to our makeshift mattress and the dozing wolf. We settle in our little manger, me on my back, Jake curled up on his side, his face nestled under my arm. I don't think it takes him more than ninety seconds to find sleep.

I feel a sense of relief as I listen to his breathing slow and grow deeper, clinging to the quiet rhythmic snore in the growing darkness. I can feel myself losing the battle to stay awake, but I desperately want to keep watch over Jake.

What little energy I have left is churning in my brain, trying to piece together the day's events. What happened today does not feel, natural, somehow. I have this feeling of impending doom in my gut, although I have not, and will not, share my fears with Jake.

I reach down with my free hand and touch the top of Achille's head. He stirs, lets out a big sigh, and he's gone again. They are safe, both of them. My mind is beginning to play tricks on me, the fatigue must be overwhelming my faculties.

Just as my eyes betray me, carry me away from this plight, I would swear I see two angry yellow eyes looking down from directly above, leering at me through the branches of our new tree.

Chapter 8

'For nothing is hidden that will not be made manifest, nor is anything secret that will not be known and come to light.'

—Luke 8:17 (ESV)

Pedro looks around the lab, mixed emotions swirling at the stark change in atmosphere. The haphazard files have all been collected, alphabetized and stored in the filing cabinets along the east wall, textbooks and reference manuals organized along new sturdy, practical bookshelves installed some weeks ago. Not a dirty coffee cup or trail of food scraps to be found on table or floor.

He scans the room, desperately looking for something, anything, to tether it, and him, to Dr. Castillo. He spots the professor's worn-out desk and threadbare chair relegated to a recess in the far back corner. It's better than nothing.

He runs his good hand along the clean surface of the desk, all signs of disarray removed. Pedro hesitates, and then rounds the desk and slowly lowers himself down. A memory of Dr. Castillo surfaces; leaning precariously far back into this rickety old chair trailing crumbs from his half-eaten sandwich from his desktop to his lap. It feels so familiar, Pedro reaches for the reminiscence.

The desk is crammed against the wall although there is nothing but empty space back here. It irritates Pedro, feels like a slight somehow. He *talks* to his electromechanical hand, still a work in progress, the muscles in his arm engaging with the microprocessors in the prosthetic.

He watches as the limb turns face up and cups the edge of the desktop with dead fingers. Without any sensory feedback, he visually checks the placement of his hand.

Not bad, he tells himself, *I'm getting better*.

Satisfied, he mirrors the position with his left hand and pushes gently against the desk. The palm from the artificial limb slips with the pressure and he careens face-first into the desk.

He lets out an exasperated, "*omph*," and the tiniest curse escapes along with it.

He doesn't feel, but rather, hears a faint click. A slim drawer springs free from under the lip of the desktop. He never would have seen it, or the secret latch he inadvertently disengaged, even had he been looking for one. The drawer is so slim it might hold a handful of paper at most.

Curious, Pedro extends the drawer to the limit of the slides on either side. At the very back of the drawer, a nondescript manila folder hides in plain sight.

Pedro ponders the peculiarity of the find. Dr. Castillo was always so, well, careless, with his materials. It is most likely just an empty folder that made its way into this long-forgotten secret drawer.

Pedro is about to close the drawer but instead, finds himself reaching in for the folder, feeling foolish, nosy, and even a little discourteous at the same time. He does it anyway.

With the folder in hand, he looks at the clock, and then the door. He is not expecting anyone for at least another hour, maybe more. His eyes slide back to the folder sitting on the desk, beckoning him. He opens it to find a torn envelope addressed to Dr. Castillo along with a single sheet of paper behind it.

He cannot stop now. He peers inside the envelope, another single sheet of paper, neatly folded. He retrieves it and unfurls the page. A poem, no, a riddle, written in the hand of a child.

The last of 12, the fourth of four,
The words that serve as proof,
Second prime plus one times two, reduce by half, repeat,
A little quest, a little toil,
But here you'll find the truth.

Uhm, more like a child prodigy. Judging by the oversized question mark scribbled on the page in red ink, Pedro assumes the professor did not solve the puzzle. He checks the envelope for a return address, but none. He checks the postmark. It was mailed from Biodome headquarters over a year and a half ago.

He had no idea Dr. Castillo was keeping secrets, he always seemed so forthcoming, so willing to share with Pedro. It stings. He looks at the second page tucked behind the envelope, recognizing the content immediately. A DNA profile. A sticky note with a hastily scrawled note, again in Dr. Castillo's unique penmanship. The note reads 'Reference sample?'

Pedro sighs. He has no need of a reference sample; he knows exactly who this sample belongs to. It is just another *tetradopophis amplectus* sample. He recognizes the repeating sequences at once, having sequenced this very sample himself when the creature was first brought to the lab.

He is just about to close the file and return it to the drawer when he eyes a single line at the bottom of the report.

Paternity confirmed.

He stops dead in his tracks. The ticking of the clock amplifies, or perhaps that is his heartbeat sounding in his head. He scans the report. Who is this? His panic is palpable. There is no name!

He looks back to the envelope, the riddle. Dr. Castillo couldn't figure out. If his brilliant teacher couldn't solve it, how can Pedro possibly expect to fare any better? The panic retreats, an inner calm pulls him back from the brink of hysteria.

He couldn't solve it because Dr. Castillo only had one perspective, one brain from which to draw conclusions. Science. But if he couldn't solve it, then science is not the answer.

Pedro pulls the sheet from the envelope, opens it, stares at it.

The last of 12.

John, the 12th apostle.

The fourth of four.

The fourth canonical gospel.
He skips over the next line.

Second prime plus one times two.

Pedro is certain this is in reference to numbers. Second prime is three, plus one is four times two is eight.

Reduce by half, repeat.

A second set of instructions within the same line, Pedro asserts. Half of eight is four, repeat, four.

Pedro assimilates the clues, interpreted through faith, Dr. Castillo's blind spot. And there lies the truth, just as the mystery riddler promised.

He speaks the words out loud, slowly, the sound of his own voice almost foreign in his ears as he recites the passage by rote.

"The Book of John, 8:44: You are of your father the devil, and your will is to do your father's desires—"

He gasps, forces his mind to stop. Slowly, he folds the letter and returns it to the envelope, wishing he had not seen it. He squeezes his eyes shut and then opens them on the DNA report, staring at the repeating sequences until the letters blur, his mind putting the pieces together.

He sways on his feet, throws his arms wide to regain his balance, as though suddenly standing on a boat in choppy waters. He looks up. Like an apparition, the medicine man stands on the other side of the desk leaning against his walking stick, flickering in and out of existence. His voice sounds a million miles away, like an echo on the wind.

"You cannot kill the one who is already dead."

His intuition had been right from the start. Pedro always sensed something sinister, something malignant in Dr. Draeger. But this. He was sent here to destroy the Biodome. There is only one person he can trust with this revelation. He has to find Everett Steele.

What have I done? I tried to kill the devil's spawn.

Maureen Domanso had been full of questions. It had taken her some time to control the chaos that had erupted when she crashed their little soirée at the abandoned stockyard, the cabinet members scattering like scared rabbits. Once

Sandra announced to the cobwebbed rafters that she was on their side, they had begun to emerge from their hidey holes, one by one.

Maureen assured them that Sandra Steele was telling the truth, she would vouch her life on it. That seemed to settle the assembly and they sat quietly, listening, still filled with trepidation. Maureen had turned on Sandra and began interrogating her.

How did she find them?

Was she followed?

How much did she hear?

Why had she come?

Despite her asperity, Sandra sensed the woman was relieved, even glad, to see her. Sandra's no-nonsense responses were almost impressive in their candor.

"I've been following you for a week now. I am alone, I am certain of it. I heard everything."

And to the last question, "Why am I here?" she half laughed.

"It seems to me you are in dire need of a sacrificial lamb. Here I am."

The chaos had come to an abrupt halt, replaced with astonished silence. Gary was first to blink, he opened his mouth, about to ask what they were all thinking when Maureen stopped him short.

"We will convene for the night. I know I don't need to remind you that discretion is paramount. Remember, it's business as usual. Sandra and I have much to discuss."

They had locked eyes, Maureen silently pleading her not to answer the unasked question. She already knew the answer, it was the same reason she was about to offer herself up. The others need not be privy to their shared misery.

She sits on the front porch, Evander and Gordon relieving her of dish duty tonight. Both husband and son have given her a wide berth lately, mistaking her reticence for lingering grief. She watches the steam swirl off her teacup, curling into the air and tickling her nose with the scent of jasmine.

Her visit to the Domanso home plays over and over in her head, on a loop. Maureen's genuine surprise at news of Everett's passing, the woman's confusion as she frantically searched the Biodome database, her pronouncement that Everett's righting protocol is not logged and therefore, never happened.

And her last words, still ringing in her ears, "Just like Jake."

But she can't quite quell the feeling that the woman had left something unsaid. She knew more.

She has said nothing of this to Gordon. It seems cruel to instill even a sliver of hope. As much as she tries to reason with herself that there is some explanation that Everett is gone, she *saw* her die, her heart has latched onto Maureen Domanso's words like a shipwrecked sailor clinging to a life raft. *It never happened.*

When everyone had left the abattoir, she had lashed out at Maureen like a scorpion, backing her into a blood-stained table.

"It's him, isn't it? Dr. Draeger has Everett."

Maureen had taken a moment to compose herself before responding.

"I don't know if he has her. I do know that he wanted, or wants, her eliminated."

"How do you know this? Why? Why would my nineteen-year-old daughter be any kind of threat to Vladimir Draeger, the most powerful agent in the Biodome?"

Sandra stood impatiently, wondering if the other woman would even deign to respond.

"I don't *know* why," she looked at Sandra's narrowed eyes, "that is the truth," she had insisted.

She continued.

"But I *do* know it to be true because I was ordered to remove her. He afforded me certain protections from EV to do the job."

She said this with such matter of fact she may as well have been reporting the weather. It made Sandra's blood boil. Before she could control her actions, she had slapped Maureen, hard, across the face, stinging her hand, leaving an angry red handprint on the woman's cheek. The other woman's pomposity evaporated.

"I did *not* go through with it," Maureen insisted, emphasizing the negative.

"But you thought about it," Sandra spat at her, turned on her heel, and stormed out.

Sandra was afforded no such *protections*. The violence against Maureen Domanso had come with a cost. Sandra has been under the weather all week, hiding her fever and chills behind excuses about having to retire early to prepare for a meeting or to complete a report. Stern as it was, by this, the third day, she is beginning to feel the righting protocol run its course.

The tea helps, she thinks, as she brings the cup to her lips. She puts the cup down on the porch side table and examines her hand. She can still feel the sting of the slap. It paled in comparison to the sting of learning that the woman who had stood before her was Everett's would-be assassin. It was worth every ache and pain.

Chapter 9

'Something wicked this way comes.'

—William Shakespeare, Macbeth

He is curled around a knot on a large, low-hanging branch, tiny claws digging into the tough bark of the mahogany tree. He is vexed. So, she has come. She must have administered healing compounds with incredible competency for the boy looks to be recovering from his lethal venom.

He rebukes himself; He should have held on a little longer, flooded the boy's system with his toxin. He was caught off guard, reactionary. He had chosen his son in a rare moment of panic. A moment of weakness. And now this.

His prey is not only going to endure, but he just became that much harder to subdue, especially with the Waheela at their side. No, this is definitely no longer a level playing field. He will have to even the odds.

He listens as the girl finally drifts off, the last holdout of the trio. At least the wolf is wounded, that should slow him down for the time being. He slinks down the trunk of the tree, crosses the stream to the wasteland on the other side, little hiccups of steam still pushing through the black crust.

Good, still warm, it will make the task ahead easier. It will weaken his bond with Vlad, but the girl and the preternatural wolf complicate matters. He is in need of a warrior of his own.

He retraces his path up the mountain, halting at a particularly thick deposit of magma that has seeped into a deep depression along the precipice. Yes, this will do. He summons the fire, it obeys like a well-trained soldier, rising from the depths.

He concentrates the flames under the pocket of molten rock, watches as the pool of magma turns from obsidian to an angry burnt orange. He releases the heat and draws on all his latent power of creation, remnants of his time at the

Other's side before He was cast out. True, He cannot create life, but He can tether his own to his creation. And so, He begins.

Human-like, He decides, but larger, more powerful. Not so big though that his own vitality is robbed, He must share his life force. He enervates his link with Vlad, He will need the extra energy to animate his warrior. It is only a temporary measure, just until He finishes his work here.

Once the bond is partially severed, He feels the surge, like a jolt of electricity travelling through his anfractuous body. The lava swirls, big lazy bubbles erupting at the surface, like a witch's brew in a cauldron.

It rises from the pool of liquified stone, eight feet tall, with legs like tree trunks, shoulders almost as wide as its height. Rudimentary facial features; it will have to intuit through its master. See through his eyes, smell through his forked tongue, hear through his sense of vibration. A magma golem.

He surveys his work, inspecting the creature as it stands at attention. As the magma cools, it loses all hint of color until it blends perfectly with the backdrop of pillowy rock. Camouflage, an added bonus He had not even considered.

Let us see what you can do, shall we?

First, He lashes his tongue, picks up the scent of burning flesh and fur to his left, a large animal that did not escape the onslaught. The golem responds, lifting its massive head and swiveling on a lumbering neck in the direction of the odor.

Next, He listens, his somatic hearing picking up the ground vibration of a smattering of loose stones as it stumbles down a ridge west of the border of the magma flow. The golem tilts its head, points the rough protuberance on the left side of its featureless face vaguely resembling a human pinna, exactly where He sensed the miniature landslide.

Next, He dilates his vertical pupils as He looks up into the sun, spotting a falcon circling high up in the orb of light. And again, the golem responds by mimicking his movements, his stone face turning upward into the blue sky. Excellent. One final test then.

He creates the scene in his mind, imagines himself picking up a massive boulder, wielding it over his head, hurling it down the mountain. The golem repeats the sequence. It chooses what looks to be a glacial erratic, impossibly large, half encased in magma, tears it free from its volcanic prison as easily as pulling a weed from a garden. Lifts it overhead, takes a few giant steps to build momentum and pitches it. The boulder seems to defy gravity for a brief moment, travelling in an upward arc before crashing to the ground and steamrolling everything in its path on its descent.

He is most pleased although the physical animation draws far more energy than simple sensory control. He feels it waver, like electricity flickering in a lightning storm. He will need to choose his targets wisely and pace himself.

He reverses course, heading back toward the stream. The golem lumbers behind him on an invisible leash, breaking through the outer shell of the molten rock with each step, like walking through freshly fallen snow. He takes them back to the flowing water, to the boy and girl and their recently acquired companion upstream.

The golem follows his glare to the opposite bank. Nothing. Still sheltering under the cover of trees then. Fortunately, they must have been to the water and back already. A window has presented itself. He sets his golem to work uprooting trees and strategically placing stones. The work takes longer than anticipated. He finds himself needing short spurts of repose, frequently enfeebled from mobilizing his Frankenstein.

Multiple layers of felled trees later, interspersed with stones and mud, He clambers atop his masterpiece. The stream is reduced to a trickle, and then finally, to nothing as his dam diverts the water toward the toxic volcanic rock bed. It begins to pool in shallow, steaming puddles. What does not evaporate absorbs the geochemical properties of the komatiite. Within minutes, the pools are polluted with heavy metals, turning the water a sickly green color.

Now that He has cut them off from the west, they will have to move east in search of food and a new water source. He scampers across the dry creek bed, the golem in tow.

It almost straddles the bed, leaving only two depressions in the soft mud from its footfalls, murky water seeping into the holes from the saturated ground. He leads them due east of the children's little encampment, assuming they will head this way when they discover there is no water.

They walk for miles, zigzagging across the landscape, searching. His diligence is rewarded when they reach a lagoon, spring-fed and crystal clear. A small ripple on the surface indicates the location of the underground source. The boy cannot be allowed to stumble upon this life-giving haven.

He spies the solution to this little conundrum, resting at the bottom of the pond. Shoring up his strength, He sets the golem to work. It walks out to the middle of the basin, the water covering the stone beast up to its waist.

Reaching down, head submersed, it fishes out a massive flagstone, flat on top and bottom with jagged edges all the way around. It is larger than the golem's torso, He is dizzy with the exertion.

Precariously close to losing his grip on the golem, He reaches down deep and feels the energy leaching out of every fiber in this wretched body. Just a few more steps.

He centers the golem over the spring and sets the flagstone directly over top, bearing down to recess it into the sandy base. It seals the spring as easily as corking a vintage wine bottle. Following the path of least resistance, the underground water will flow right past the spring, the pond should dry up in a matter of days. In the interim, stagnation will ensure it is no longer potable.

He releases the golem, it stands perfectly still, inanimate. Without his lifeforce, it looks like a king-size inukshuk. He clambers up to the leg and torso to the shoulder and fans himself out in the sun. He needs a little siesta to replenish himself, there is more work to do.

Draeger rests comfortably in his posh leather recliner, working out the details of the plan with his assistant. Like all great dominions, the status quo is never enough, it is time to squeeze a little harder and tighten the vice. Wring a bit more out of the citizenry, just to ensure the people do not become too comfortable or complacent.

He must remind them that they are powerless. And then he will throw them a bone or two, naturally they will be eternally grateful for his munificence. The same old play from the tried-and-true gamebook of human politics. It never gets old.

The map of the Biodome is splayed across the little conference table in the corner of his office. Maureen Domanso is placing colored markers over land and water, the map transforming into a bingo card. She picks up a yellow marker, rolling the little plastic game piece between her index finger and thumb. He clucks his tongue at her.

"Ah ah, remember, we are nothing if not fair. I already see three yellows on the board."

Three yellows, three blues, three greens, only two reds, only one purple. She replaces the yellow with a purple, her former stomping ground, the department of health promotion. Yellow, representing the department of agriculture, blue, for fisheries and oceans, and green, animal welfare, were all easy targets.

"Having a hard time with your old alma mater deary?" he teases.

"Not at all Sir," she returns.

All business.

"It is one thing to regulate arable land and navigable waters, and I've even been able to map out the planned power outages, but I am finding it quite another matter altogether to restrict access to health services for innocent children and newborns."

Does he detect a hint of condescension in her tone? Insubordination even? She seems to snap out of it.

"Sorry Sir, I am just frustrated. Here." She places the purple marker on the map.

"There is a large urban center in the southeast quadrant, it is chronically under capacity. We can wrest control right here," she taps the marker for emphasis.

That's better. He peruses the map, satisfied with the dispersion of sanctions and cutbacks. He counts the targets. Lucky thirteen.

"Very well, Ms. Domanso. Do keep me apprised as each of our new measures is implemented. Of course, the full force of the state media is at your disposal to remind the people of their duty to the Biodome. Incidentally, what are the latest infection rates? Anything interesting?"

With her customary proficiency, Maureen produces the latest quarterly report, graphed by quadrant.

"Not really, typical pre-agent activity, mostly mild variants. The young and foolish, they will soon learn. Would you like to review the data?" She brandishes the document, the bar graphs flashing in and out of Draeger's view.

"No, it is as it should be. I do find it rather amusing though how new humans always stick their hand in the fire at least once. It must be a compulsion. Knowing full well they are going to get burned but alas…always needing to test the waters for themselves. Some things never change."

He reminisces about ancient times when governments spent billions of dollars on campaigns that warned youth about the dangers of smoking, vaping, drinking and illicit drug use, all falling on deaf ears. The irony is so rich, he is almost jealous of what they managed to accomplish. Decrying these ancient proclivities all the while sanctioning, even subsidizing, their manufacture and profiting handsomely from their widespread consumption.

The blank stare on his assistant's face brings him back to the moment.

"That will be all, Ms. Domanso."

With the unceremonious dismissal, she moves to dismantle the map.

"No, that you will leave as it is until the plan is in full motion."

"Of course, Sir," she curtsies just a little, but not fast enough to hide a flash as her eyes narrow uncontrollably.

He senses unmistakable hatred in those eyes as she turns to go.

Jake works the knots out, twisting his back this way and that, stretching limbs against the tree. He pulls gently on his jaw until his neck cracks, relieving some of his lingering discomfort. Everett is still sleeping, curled up against Achilles' side. He won't wake them.

He tugs at his earlobe with one hand while he walks toward the creek, eager to ease his thirst and rinse the grit from his eyes. The ringing is gone, but there is a little throb deep inside the ear. The morning gets eerily quiet as he approaches the stream, the sound of chirping and rustling all but gone.

The wildlife will be moving east, away from the ravaged land to the west of the stream. A sinking feeling overwhelms him as he thinks about the creatures that did not make it to safety yesterday.

Jake rubs his eyes while he walks. His tired brain must be playing tricks on him. There, in the distance. He could swear the ground is moving; little flashes of silver reflected in the sun. What the…he squints, cranes his neck forward, trying to focus. He increases his pace, never taking his eyes from the shifting terrain ahead.

That sinking feeling intensifies when he reaches the stream. No water. Just hundreds of silvery minnows, tiny little eyes staring helplessly, mouths opening and closing in desperation, flopping around the dry creek bed. More lay perfectly still. Jake turns away and closes his eyes.

The stream was fine yesterday, the volcanic flow did not reach this far. Why? He walks upstream until he spies a massive dam diverting the water. He follows the flow directly into the billowy lava and dips a hand in a pool between pillows. The water is warm and greenish. He brings his hand to his nose and scrunches his face up at the sulphury smell.

Jake returns to the dam and inspects it more closely. Trees and rocks layered expertly, even clay chinking to seal the holes. Something worthy of the Department of Engineering and Infrastructure. Something man-made.

He whips his head around; realization hits him like a slap. He starts at a sprint, back to Everett, his aching joints forgotten. He has only one thought as he crashes through the underbrush. *We are not alone.*

Chapter 10

'But evil men and imposters will grow worse and worse, deceiving and being deceived.'

—2 Timothy 3:13 (NJKV)

Maureen paces the boardroom floor, head down, hands clenched, mumbling to herself.

Is this a bloody game to him? Does his rapacity know no bounds? He's gone too far this time. Children? Really?

As the cabinet members begin to shuffle in one by one, she checks her outrage and smooths her features. She must retain control of her emotions, lest she add to the tension of a cabinet already taut as a bowstring. When everyone is seated and the fidgeting subsides, she faces her colleagues.

"I appreciate the difficulty of our situation, but we must stay the course. The plan is unchanged, Sandra Steele has not changed her mind."

Gary clears his throat.

"That is all well and good, but what do we do in the meantime? Sneaking around behind his back seems ill-advised, but this? Right under his nose? This is madness."

Maureen grimaces. She grits her teeth.

"What would you have us do Gary, disappear in the middle of the day to our little rendezvous point in the woods? That won't raise suspicion, not at all."

She pauses for effect. "Better we meet right here, business as usual, remember? It is imperative we keep up appearances."

Agents nod in agreement. Maureen takes that as her cue to continue.

"Very well then. The annual conference is too far away, we must find a reason to assemble sooner. I have an idea. He has a new plan. He wants more sanctions, more cutbacks, more restrictions. Thirteen new targets."

She puts a hand up to stop the inevitable protests. Red faces, sputtering, hands slapping the tabletop; the room is about to explode. Just then, the door opens. Dr. Draeger, brows raised, lips slightly pursed, walks slowly into the boardroom. He looks at Maureen.

"It seems I've been overlooked on the invite list. Ms. Domanso, have you forgotten your duties as my personal assistant?"

The air feels thin in Maureen's lungs. He must be following her. Does he suspect? Does he know? She thought she was being so careful. Did she give herself away somehow? Her brain scrambles for a plausible explanation.

"Of course not, Sir. It is only that I did not want to waste your time with the minutiae of the new plan. That is what we are all here for after all."

She sweeps a hand across the room at the blank faces, her eyes silently invoking corroboration. Gary picks up the mantel.

"Yes, Ms. Domanso was just explaining the plan. Thirteen targets I believe? Brilliant. We were just about to get to the nitty-gritty, Sir."

Maureen holds her breath. Draeger is no fool, he knows something is amiss.

Do. Not. Cave. she scolds herself. She lifts her chin and looks directly at him. Any sign of duplicity now will mean the end of all of them. Odd, she thinks, suddenly he looks quite weary. Exhausted even. His hand goes to his throat to loosen the tie at his neck, most un-Draeger like. He reaches for an empty chair and drops into it without any of his customary refinement.

The agents around the table have noticed as well, most are smart enough to look away. Henry fusses with a thread on the sleeve of his cardigan, Paul rubs furiously at his glasses with a tissue, Edith inspects her manicure and begins picking at her nails. Maureen capitalizes on the moment, seizing the opportunity to get back into his good graces.

"We've wasted enough of Dr. Draeger's time today. See to it that you read the brief that I've sent you, you will be expected to explain your tactical maneuvers at the next meeting," she huffs. "Well, what are you waiting for? To your assignments."

She waves to the door.

The agents scramble to their feet, collecting their belongings in haste and depart single file, eagerness writ large in every step. Maureen is the last to leave, glancing back at Draeger, sprawled in the chair, looking much, much worse for wear.

Could it be a righting protocol? Is he finally getting his due? How serendipitous. Any lingering doubts about him are swept away as she turns her back and mouths a silent "thank you" to the Biodome as the door clicks behind her.

A flash of red dances across the mirror as Draeger rifles through the neatly pressed dress shirts hanging perfectly spaced in the massive walk-in closet. Arranged by color, white to black, with pastels to bold hues in between.

He stands midway, his hand hovering somewhere in the blues. He glances over his shoulder at the mirror, the shimmery scales move like liquid across his back. It always makes him think of Father. What He must endure. At least his own transformation is only partial. A small blessing.

He decides on royal blue, moving to his tie rack and choosing a deep gold to compliment the shirt. Clean-shaven, coiffed, and now dressed like an ancient James Bond, he was always fond of that character, he heads to the kitchen.

Wall to wall, floor to ceiling windows overlooking the East River, he's just minutes from headquarters. He reclaimed this penthouse for his personal use; no need to live like the masses. Class warfare was a hallmark of the ancients, everyone tripping over the other for wealth and status.

He chuckles inwardly at the ancient middle-class obsession with, what was it again? Oh yes, keeping up with the Joneses. Even better though, the public feuds between rival billionaires living the ultra-lavish lifestyles of the rich and famous while families lined up at foodbanks around city blocks and even more returned home to their tents in the streets. Just as it should be.

The aroma of freshly brewed coffee fills the open space with undertones of chocolate and cranberry that tickle at his taste buds as he takes his first sip. Cup in hand, he stands at the bank of windows, staring at the water as it ripples past, savoring the intensity of the brew.

Sleep has not abated the nagging suspicion that something is amiss with Maureen Domanso. She is as competent as ever, but he has been at this for a very long time. This one is hard to read, but he is not mistaken, her mask slipped yesterday, just for a second. Time for a little reconnaissance of his own.

He walks to headquarters today. The air is cool and crisp against his face, exactly what he needs to clear his head. He decides to pay his assistant a little impromptu visit this morning, gauge her reaction and observe closely. She is good, but she does have tells. She will brush her hair behind her ear if she is nervous, avert her eyes if she is holding her tongue.

The walk is uneventful and before he knows it, Draeger is stepping into his office on the fifth floor. He spies the map still covering the conference table and takes a moment to scan the targets. Father will be pleased with his progress. He thinks wistfully at the short time he held the existential virus in the palm of his hand. To hold on to so much power was admittedly intoxicating. This play-acting might be working, but it pales by comparison. His unavoidable reliance on humans leaves much to be desired.

He sighs, there is nought to be done for it. Speaking of which, time to call on Ms. Domanso, the human who holds more power than she comprehends. To think, it all comes down to the whims of a mundane woman. Best to be absolutely certain her loyalties are well placed.

His first surprise of the day only fuels his circumspection. An archiving agent sits at the administration desk outside Domanso's office, fingers flying over the keys as he organizes Domanso's records in the Biodome's intricate indexed sequential filing system.

So engrossed in his task, Draeger slips right by without notice. The knock at Domanso's door gets the agent's attention. The tapping stops as he looks up and nearly knocks his chair over when he bolts to his feet. He fumbles, words coming out one at a time, one syllable at a time.

"Oh, Sir. Yes. Well."

Draeger arches an eyebrow at the agent, somewhere near retirement he suspects, clearly not good at small talk. Or talking in general. He knocks again. The agent strings together a partially cohesive message.

"Uhm, Sir. Ms. Domanso is not in. I mean, she's in, she's here, but not in her office."

Draeger waits. When the agent fails to elaborate, the irritation is evident in his voice.

"Speak. Where is she then?"

The agent looks like he wants to nosedive under the bureau. Draeger does seem to have that effect on humans.

"Ugh, she is in the boardroom, Sir."

"There, that was not so difficult now, was it? As you were."

The agent nearly misses the chair on his way down, stumbling backwards just in time to recover. Draeger is too preoccupied to be annoyed. He marches straight to the boardroom and ploughs through the closed door. The entire cabinet is assembled, they sit wide-eyed, staring at him in the doorway. As though they've been caught red-handed.

"It seems I've been overlooked on the invite list yet again. Ms. Domanso, have you forgotten your duties as my personal assistant?"

He watches her closely. Nothing to indicate any wrongdoing.

"Of course not, Sir. It is only that I did not want to waste your time with the minutiae of the new plan. That is what we are all here for, after all."

A slight pause and then the DOA agent confirms.

"Yes, Sir. Ms. Domanso was just explaining the plan. Thirteen targets I believe? Brilliant. We were just about to get to the nitty-gritty, Sir."

He is still reading the room when a wave of dizziness washes over him, threatening to take his feet out from under him. The link is so weak as to be imperceptible, the life force draining, barely a trickle. As if Father is cutting him off. No, that is not it. Father is expending so much energy he cannot sustain the connection.

The vertigo is paralyzing; he can only watch as Domanso takes control and ushers everyone out of the room. She has the good grace to exercise discretion for herself as well, taking one look back at him, a combination of confusion and disbelief, before she too, disappears behind the door. Any lingering doubts about her are swept away. Her loyalty is unassailable.

Gradually the disorientation fades, his senses sharpen. Like a giant elastic band rebounding after being stretched to its breaking point, the connection with Father is restored, leaving him physically exhausted but otherwise unscathed. No need to waste more time on unfounded suspicions about Domanso. She proved herself again today, jumpstarting the new plan first thing after finalizing the targets.

Her only crime is her zeal, her lust for power. She protected him today, shielded him in an unwonted moment of vulnerability. Much better to spend his time on his real enemies. Like the urchin who disfigured him. Where is the Ramón boy anyway and what is he up to these days?

He stands, removes any signs of dishevelment, tucking and smoothing, aligning. Satisfied, Draeger squares his shoulders and exits the boardroom with the crisp gait of a five-star general.

Chapter 11

'I knew that I was dying,
Something inside me said.
go ahead, die, sleep, become
as them, accept.
then something else inside me said, no,
save the tiniest bit.
it needn't be much,
just a spark.
a spark can set a whole forest on fire.
just a spark.
save it.'

—Charles Bukowski

Pedro stares out the oval window, remembering the last time he sat in an aircraft, the body of Dr. Castillo in the cargo hold being returned home for interment.

The old feelings come rushing back despite his best effort to tamp them down. The grief fueled the rage that fueled the need to exact justice for his mentor. A grave mistake that has made him the enemy of the penultimate enemy.

Senhora Everett will know what to do. They have faced insuperable trials before and somehow prevailed. They can do it again. If they cannot kill him, at least they can neutralize him. If Pedro has learned one thing from all of this, it is that Vladimir Draeger is not entirely without vulnerabilities. They will find a way.

He is still deliberating when the plane touches down, bouncing lightly along the runway as the aviation agent works to slow the vessel's momentum. The plane comes to a stop in front of a building with windows that bulge slightly in the center. Blue sky and clouds reflect in the mirrored glass panels that cover the entire north wall.

This Midwest airport is more modest than the one at Biodome headquarters, which suits Pedro just fine. He easily navigates the terminal with his overnight bag slung over one shoulder.

Officially, he is here to collect samples from the Midwestern DAW apiary as part of the new apitherapy program. He insisted on procuring the beeswax, pollen, propolis, royal jelly, and venom samples himself, scientific integrity and all that.

It was his idea to include the northwest quadrant in the program. No one has to know that the entire project was contrived to give him a legitimate excuse to see Everett Steele in person.

Fifty-three minutes later, the shuttle bus deposits him outside the main administration building of the DAW. A detailed map of the sprawling campus is smartly affixed to the brick wall adjacent to the main door. He plays back his first encounter with Everett in his mind. It was the annual conference; they had exchanged pleasantries standing in the grass.

"You're a long way from home," she had observed.

"*Si, senhora*, I am Pedro Ramón. I am from the Department of Education and Research, southwest quadrant, northeast campus."

"Wow, fancy Pedro. I'm Everett, Everett Steele, I'm here with my mom but I'm in animal welfare, Midwest campus. Horses and wolves are kind of my thing."

Pedro studies the map for a moment, pleased to locate the equine program not far from where he stands, not so thrilled to learn that the lupus program is at the opposite end of the complex. He will definitely try equine first in hopes of finding her there. He is so preoccupied with Everett Steele, he almost forgets to locate the apiary. More good fortune today, it is not far from the stables.

He registers as a department guest, declining the escort offered to him.

"*Nao, Senhor*, that is not necessary. I do not wish to make a fuss."

The paths are well-marked with friendly signs in the shape of animals pointing the way. He chuckles at the goofy-looking walrus sign guiding him toward the equine compound. It is a short-lived reprieve from the despondency bearing down on him.

As Pedro hikes along the well-worn trail, he cradles the leather bag lying across his chest protectively. His fingers play with the little indents in the leather pocket, a habit he's developed. Proof that his time with Everett inside the Biodome was not a dream. A reminder of how close those fangs had come to finding flesh. The bag now holds the truth about Dr. Draeger. Who he is. What he is.

He reaches equine administration after a short but brisk walk, his pace fast enough to produce a bead of sweat along his hairline. He sweeps a hand across his forehead as he enters the small building and presents his visitor's badge to the agent sitting behind a large desk, the wall behind her wallpapered with posters of horses.

She flashes Pedro a brilliant white smile that brings a flush to his cheeks and adds to the heat on his brow. A charming cowgirl twang colors her words, conjuring images of daisies and bluebells in his mind.

"Why hello there, haven't seen you around these parts before. How can I help ya' all sugar?"

The flirtation in her voice disarms him for the briefest second, only long enough for memories of Morning Sun to surface and slam the door. All business.

"*Olá, bom dia*, good morning. I was hoping to speak with a department agent, Everett Steele?"

He had not intended for his request to sound like a question. The agent pouts her bottom lip, seemingly disappointed in his interest in a female agent. She regains her bubbly disposition with a quick shrug and a puff of air that rustles her bangs.

"Of course, sugar. I'm new here, don't know everyone just yet. Let ol' Cassie here finds her for ya'." She grabs the computer mouse and begins rolling and tapping.

"Uhm, thank you, Cassie," Pedro says, amused by her peculiar vernacular.

An exaggerated frown grows on her pretty face as she scrolls through her computer screen.

"Well darlin', I see she *was* here, but it's lookin' like she's been gone a while now."

Gone? Pedro is surprised by this development.

"I see," he says slowly. "Can you tell me where she transferred?"

A smooth baritone voice from behind him prickles his skin with gooseflesh. He recognizes it instantly.

"I am afraid Cassandra cannot help you, Mr. Ramón. Ms. Steele has not transferred anywhere. She is in fact, gone."

Cassie's radiance is quashed like a bug on a windshield. She is suddenly small, caving in on herself, sinking deeper into her chair. She looks positively downtrodden, a little bird with clipped wings.

She peeks up at Pedro who gives her a reassuring look before turning to face Dr. Draeger. Draeger looks him up and down, his eyes landing on his right hand, a wicked smirk on his lips, there and gone. He tilts his chin slightly to one side and nods in approval.

"We must catch up, Mr. Ramón. Walk with me. I believe the apiary agents are awaiting your arrival."

Pedro would rather walk on hot coals, but he is cornered. Draeger must be tracking him, surveying his movements. He just said as much. How else could he know why he is here? What else does he know? Does he know about the familial DNA report? He clutches the leather satchel instinctively.

"*Si*, thank you, Dr. Draeger, lead the way."

He follows a few steps behind, staring at the doctor's back. Picturing the scar parallel to the spinal column underneath the suit jacket and fancy-dress shirt. His hand automatically curls dead, mechanical fingers around an imaginary scalpel.

Pedro needs to ask about Everett. He is rallying the courage to demand information when Draeger breaks the silence as though reading his thoughts.

"You wish to know where Miss Steele has gone," Draeger states curiously, not bothering to turn around to address him.

"*Si*," he clears his throat.

Draeger continues to lead him toward the melittology lab, the droning of thousands of bees piercing the silence as they approach.

"Interesting, your itinerary makes no mention of meetings outside the new apitherapy project."

That is all the confirmation Pedro needs. Draeger is definitely following him. He attempts to trivialize the visit.

"No meeting. I just thought to stop by and see a friend while I am here, that is all."

"Yes, how propitious that you should find yourself here of all places, by mere happenstance no less."

Draeger's tone is light, but the underlying message is clear. He knows this is no coincidence. Now he feels the need to justify the visit.

"The Midwest campus has one of the largest ground nesting sites in the Biodome. We do not have access to carpenter bees and nomads in the southeast quadrant. This was the obvious choice," he declares with a hint of indignation to mask the fear clawing its way to the surface.

"Of course. I am a bit of an *Anthophila* aficionado myself. Such industrious little creatures, going about their own business. So laissez faire. Unless provoked that is."

Pedro cringes inwardly, the veiled threat crawling up his spine. Draeger is watching him now. Like a cat about to pounce. He tugs on the shoulder strap of his bag, snugging it up tight across his chest, as if that will somehow protect the secret inside. Draeger lets the message linger a moment and then continues.

"Please, allow me to acquaint you with the hives."

He steps into a gated compound, completely sealed in a cellophane-like material, air exchangers whirring on either end. An aptly colored yellow sign with bold black writing posted on the entranceway reads:

APIARY AGENTS ONLY
DOUBLE LAYER BEE SUIT MANDATORY

Pedro gapes at Draeger who saunters into the compound without a care in the world. The doctor quirks an eyebrow at him, following his gaze.

"A superfluous precaution. There is no danger so long as we do not disturb the nests."

Pedro steps inside slowly, a grid of well-worn pathways running east and west, north and south, the length of the enclosure. The earthen squares in between are filled with thousands of tiny mounds of soil, a void in the center of each one.

Each burrow feeds into an intricate system of tunnels leading to a cabalistic megalopolis. Directly under his feet. He raises on to tiptoe at the thought, suddenly wishing he was more insubstantial.

"Forgive my skepticism. You are correct, this is the obvious choice," Draeger waves his hand across the three-acre grid.

"We have dozens of species living together, thriving even. We estimate there are over half a million busy bodies toiling away underfoot as we speak."

Pedro raises himself off the balls of his feet now, balancing precariously on cramped toes. Draeger chuckles.

"You need not worry. If you pay them no mind, they will return the sentiment. Leave and let be."

Pedro catches the pun. He does not find it amusing.

There is a little outpost building at the end of the main pathway. Draeger continues walking toward the shack.

"You can collect your samples in the safety of the field lab, it is fully stocked," he offers casually.

Pedro looks at the little building, gauging how many steps he has to take before reaching the sanctuary. Too many.

"Oh dear, how careless of me. I've forgotten my passkey. We will need it to access the lab. I will get the bypass code from Dr. Levine. Wait here."

Not waiting for a response, Draeger brushes up against Pedro as he doubles back to retrieve the key, slowing his movement when their bodies make contact.

The air dims for a moment, Pedro watches the world fade to a monochromatic grey, blurring at the edges as though his vision were being siphoned off. He blinks several times, wondering if the stress of the situation is playing tricks on his mind.

The doctor's voice breaks the spell.

"The ancients had such a penchant for trivial records. Humans immortalized for suffering the most broken bones, or for having the longest hair, or for having eaten the most this or that in one sitting."

A brief pause and he continues.

"They even celebrated the humans who survived the most bee stings, strange as that sounds. If I recall, it was a fellow working in a tin mine somewhere in the southeast quadrant, stung some 2443 times."

Draeger's remarks are easy-going, conversational, as he makes his way to the gate.

He unlocks the gate and exits the compound, dropping the lock back into place. He turns to look directly at Pedro.

"You are quite the busybody yourself, Mr. Ramón. Not one to shy away from a challenge, no matter how formidable. No problem poking the bear. Or the nest," Draeger muses, his voice taking on a dangerous, almost maniacal edge.

He crouches and places the palm of his hand flat on the ground. The earth begins to rumble under his feet. Pedro watches in horror as the land surrounding him on all sides begins to erupt with ornery airborne mercenaries, pouring out from a thousand burrows. He hears Draeger one last time over the growing din of the angry mob.

"Now, if you will excuse me, I have called a meeting of my apiary agents at central administration. I shan't be discourteous and leave them waiting. Not to worry, the team will be back tomorrow morning, bright and early. In the meantime, let's see if you can outdo the ancients."

Pedro's first instinct is to make a run for the door, although he knows it will be locked. He forces himself to absolute stillness, any movement will only embolden the growing swarm. He feels the first sting, high on his neck, behind his right ear.

He lifts his right hand instinctively, stopping short just in time to avoid injuring himself with his metallic limb. He removes the bag strewn across his chest, moving slowly, deliberately. He sits, places the bag beside him, brings his knees to his chest, drops his head between them, and tries to make himself as insignificant as possible.

The second sting goes straight through the material of his pants, stretched over his bent knee. He twitches but manages to remain static. It is all he can hear now, the hum of a million beating wings descending upon him. A million hairy little feet, all over him, tickling, infiltrating his clothing, clambering through the mess of curls to his scalp.

It is enough to drive him mad. Number three, on the middle knuckle of his left hand. Four, on the same hand, closer to the wrist. Five, on the bottom lip. Numbers floating around in his brain. Two. Four. Four. Three. 2443.

He doesn't remember moving, but he is lying on his side now, curled in the fetal position. The vertigo comes in waves, followed by roiling nausea. He peers at his own eyelashes, his eyelids swollen to bursting. How long? Hours? Or mere minutes? How many? He lost count a long, long time ago. His mind dissociates from his body. Much better.

He feels nothing. His mother's mulish face comes into focus. Always so steadfast in her opinions and principles, her tenacity etched into the lines around her eyes and mouth. It brings a smile to badly bruised, distended lips. His genteel father, quiet but sage. Pedro's biggest champion. Dr. Castillo, his image faded at the edges now, sifting away like sand washed out by the tide.

He floats, reveling in the people he loves. Feeling calm, at peace. His brain protects him from reality. His body lay in ruins, ravaged. Breaths come in disjointed gasps, his lungs trying desperately to work around a severely constricted airway.

He feels himself drifting, sleep calling to him. Yes, that will be nice, he does feel so very tired. Just as he is about to let go; to let his mind still inside this broken body, he hears his name. It is so far away; it reaches him like the echo of an echo. He strains, is he dreaming already? There it is again, a whisper on a distant wind. Beckoning him.

Pedro. Pedro, listen, hear me, come to me.

The voice elicits one final vision before the world goes black.
Everett Steele.

Chapter 12

'Water, water, everywhere, and all the boards did shrink; Water, water, everywhere, Nor any drop to drink—'
   —Samuel Taylor Coleridge, *Rime of the Ancient Mariner*

I am jolted awake. Jake is frantic, he's been running, he's panting. I can't make sense of what he is saying. Or trying to say. His yammering makes him sound like a flock of seagulls.

"Jake, slow down. One word at a time."

My head spins a little at the abrupt awakening.

"Water. No water. Dam. Someone. Someone…here."

He hacks violently, choking on his ragged breaths. I pat him gently on the back, rub up and down his spine until the racking cough subsides.

"Okay. Back up. What do you mean no water?"

It still takes him a beat to reply.

"Evey, the stream has been dammed. The water is running straight into the lava flow."

Not the end of the world. The shifting and shaking from the eruption will have undoubtedly toppled trees over, it might even have caused a mudslide. The stream was just out of reach of the eruption anyway, I was surprised it wasn't swallowed up.

"It's alright, Jake. We'll just keep moving east. There will be all kinds of water out there."

I look in the direction of the newly risen sun.

Jake looks at me like I've grown three heads.

"Everett. The stream was *dammed*."

His eyes are big as saucers.

"Yes Jake, you said that. Not all that surprising, that was a massive eruption. It could have sparked a rockslide, a landslide maybe, it will have uprooted trees for sure."

Jake is shaking his head at me.

"I found the dam, Evey. That is no calamity of nature. The dam is perfect. The dam is man-made."

Now it's my turn to stop dead in my tracks. He's nodding his head as he watches me unpack this information.

"So, what you're saying is, someone, what? Built this dam? On purpose?"

Jake's voice shakes as he professes, "Judging by the sheer scale of the dam, I'd say more like some-thing."

Achilles is already panting as we trek eastward, he has not had water since yesterday. Despite literally having just escaped death, Jake sets a grueling pace. His lean body ripples with corded muscle, his back expands with each deep, measured lungful of air.

He moves with the agility of a mountain cat. He has become the Vitruvian Man. I, on the other hand, have some catching up to do. The sweat plasters my hair against my forehead, my calves and quads feel like they are on fire, and I imagine my movements look more like a three-toed sloth than a mountain cat.

We trample through underbrush and over outcroppings and across fields of long ropey grass that tangles around my legs, trying to pull me down. It can't be more than two hours since we set out and yet I am utterly spent. And very, very thirsty. I'm just about to plop down in the middle of this pasture when Jake's head perks up. He straightens up to his full height and points over the billowing grass.

"Over there! Water!"

He starts running, Achilles bounding at his side. Really? My cramped legs protest as I attempt to pick up a lope. I settle for a slow trot, following the trampled grass Jake and the wolf left in their wake. When I finally break through and reach the water's edge, Achilles is lapping at the water like his life depends on it.

Jake is kneeling, pulling water to his face, splashing it over his head, laughing fanatically. I stick my face in the water like a horse at the trough and drink, savoring each molecule. When I come up for air, I already feel better. Until I see the look on Jake's face that is. Gone is the jubilation of a moment earlier.

"What Jake? We are safe and sound now. You look as glum as mud," I tease, trying to keep it light.

He dips his hand in the water, near the edge of the basin, brings wet fingers up to his face, rubbing his thumb against his fingertips. He smells his hand.

"It's a little, oily. And there is a slight odor," he says more to himself than to me.

I mimic his actions, dipping my hand. He's right. It has a greasy texture to it, and a musty undertone when I sniff. I didn't notice anything at first, I was so desperate to sate the thirst. But now I see a thin green film beginning to develop at the edge of the pond where the water meets the shoreline.

"I don't understand. If this is standing water, it should be a swamp. There should be reeds and sedges and Lillie pads. It would be, I don't know, swampy, wouldn't it?"

I can hear the child in my own voice.

Jake is shaking his head, his face like stone.

"I've seen these little oases all over the garden. To the west. I even have my favorite swimming hole, waterfall and all. This is, was, exactly like the others. Minus the waterfall of course," he adds. "They are spring-fed."

"So, what does that mean, Jake?" I have a sinking feeling in the pit of my stomach.

"Someone has obstructed the spring. Or something."

There is a mixture of fear and menace in his eyes as he looks at me.

"Drink now. Because in a few days, this pond will be a festering bog."

He is stretched out on a large boulder, exposing as much of himself to the sun as possible. Shoring up his strength in preparation for unleashing more havoc on this garden. The magma golem stands motionless, nothing more than an elaborate array of stones now that its life force has been diminished.

He expends just enough energy to keep its form intact, to keep it from toppling over. He'll not be needing his oversize beast for his next assault.

He'd waited, knowing they would find the little pond. Earlier than He'd hoped. The boy is becoming quite adept at living in the garden. The life-snatching bacteria and mold had just begun to grow spores when they'd happened upon the water.

No matter, it will be a quagmire in a few short days. He'll allow them to enjoy the reprieve, it will be short-lived. Feeling rejuvenated, He glides off the rock and gets to work.

He has the ancients to thank for sparking his next offensive. Without their example, He might never have appreciated the raw power of nature when manipulated just so. Even the slightest uptick in temperature can have serious consequences. Before the Other's pesky interference and radical course correction, mankind was more than willing to sacrifice their planet for power and prosperity.

He'd enjoyed the added entertainment provided by the paper-thin veneer of outrage at the demise of the global environment, regaled while pusillanimous statemen cast blame on shameful, irresponsible suburban families for driving a car and cooking with gas.

It was all going so well; the floods, the hurricanes, the droughts, the lightning storms, the glorious fires. He'd so enjoyed watching them get swallowed up by their astigmatic greed. The great chasm was so delightfully hectic in those days. So many heedless souls lined up for a little piece of real estate in Tartarus. How He longs for easier times.

He snaps out of the trance, admonishing himself for the wistful and entirely unproductive commemorations. There is work to do. He reaches deep down, the familiar pull of the flames calling him home. Not yet. He draws boundless heat from the Lake of Fire, channeling it into the atmosphere.

His cold-blooded body warms as the temperature in the garden rises. He continues to radiate heat until the bright sun rising in the east is rendered insignificant. Until it is 105 degrees in the shade.

He knows full well the Other will bring the rain. It might sustain them for a time, but it won't help with the heat. In fact, it will only add to the humidex. And besides, it is a fair trade-off. The ancients learned the hard way that disturbing the balance of nature is not so easily remedied. The rain will only bring more misery. He's counting on it.

We've set out in search of a new water source, although I'm starting to suspect we are going to be disappointed. I'm not sure if it's the exertion from the constant rambling through thick brush and occasional brambles, but I am seriously overheating. My flimsy shift is sticking to me, sweat trickling between my breasts and at the nape of my neck.

I pull my hair up into a knot on the top of my head and shove an alder branch through it to hold it in place. Jake's curls are wet, and I can see a line blooming down the center of his back. Somehow this makes me feel a bit better. With the sun dipping into the west, my guess is its past dinnertime.

"Is it my imagination Jake, or is it getting warmer? It seems to me with the sun setting, it should be cooling off and yet—" I don't finish.

"I was just thinking the same thing, Evey. It has never been this hot in the garden, at least since I've been here. It's always been quite comfortable. And this humidity. I can practically feel the water in my lungs."

"Same," is all I say in return.

I am imagining a nice tepid shower right now, but I don't share my daydream. Jake interrupts my thoughts.

"With this much humidity, it's bound to rain soon. Good thing too because I could really use a shower."

I narrow my eyes at him. I swear he *can* read my mind.

Jake is oblivious to my mental sputtering.

"Maybe we should stop for the day. There are plenty of dinner options around here. We passed through some berry bushes back there and we've got chickweed, burdock, and wild asparagus right here."

He squats down, inspecting the plants sprouting at our feet.

"Would be better boiled, but that would require…well, raw will do for tonight."

The chickweed is pleasant enough, the burdock crunches like celery but tastes a bit like the wild asparagus. A bit rooty and earthy to my palate but all in all, not half bad. And the berries are bursting with flavor, sweet and juicy. I can't complain.

Jake seems to be enjoying our little spread himself, I laugh when he shovels a handful of berries into his mouth and juice spurts through his lips and down his chin. Cute, but then, I realize he is famished, his six-foot-plus frame and broad shoulders begging for calories.

We must have put in twenty miles in the last three days. The soles of my feet ache, and every muscle in my body in the consistency of Jell-O. I can already feel sleep tugging at the edges of my consciousness even while I'm scooping up bramble berries. In synch as always, Jake yawns so wide, I think he's locked his jaw.

"I don't think I could outrun a garden snail right now," he admits, setting his left foot in his lap and kneading his thumbs between his toes.

"Did you eat enough? I mean, I know you must be thirsty but maybe the berries helped a bit with that?" Still worried about me.

"I'm fine, Jake. I have everything I need right here."

I shuffle over to him and lean my head against his shoulder. He wraps his arm around me and pulls me in and just like that, everything becomes more bearable. Achilles comes trotting through the scrub, tail and nose high in the air, licking his chops. He has that telltale glow in his eyes and dilated pupils that I've come to learn mean his hunt has produced a satisfying bounty.

He flops down beside us and starts licking at the wounded paw. He doesn't protest when I pick it up to check. The cut is closing, the margins look pink and healthy, no sign of infection. Another good note to end the day.

Grandpa always taught me that every dark cloud has a silver lining. I've just found two. I hold on to that sentiment as I settle back against Jake. He is lost in his own thoughts, talking just doesn't seem appropriate in the moment. I reach for his hand, and bringing it to my mouth, kiss it gently. Enough said. Despite everything, I fall asleep content and sleep like a baby.

It's been raining for five straight days. Jake has cleverly fashioned funnels out of tough, veiny oversized leaves connected to a makeshift drainage system that empties precious water into our homemade reservoir. We've dug out a small basin and lined it with layers of stone. It felt good to work side by side with Jake, we truly do complement one another.

Achilles appreciates our efforts, poking his nose in for a drink at regular intervals. We've also constructed a respectable shelter for ourselves. We are high and dry tucked away in a cavity between the buttress roots of a massive old palm tree.

We spend our nights under a canopy of interlaced branches we've built over the roots and thatched with leaves and pine needles. It's all we need.

The heat has not abated despite the steady downpour. There is a layer of steam twelve inches from the ground all around us reminding me of a cheesy Hallowe'en movie Evander and I watched as kids.

I swear the heat is rising from the earth. It is so intense; I can feel it radiating up my legs. I clamber up the exposed roots for a little relief. I watch the rain fall, it's not angry or vindictive, but soft, almost inviting. Falling as though it were sent to sustain us, to nourish us, when we need it most.

The combination of heat and humidity lends vitality to the garden. I can practically see the foliage growing, leaves unfurling, thick and green and supple, closing in all around us. See, not so bad, I've just found another silver lining.

Now that we've settled into this new tree, the devastation and chaos from the volcano don't feel so unnerving. In a strange way, our perseverance has only strengthened my resolve, I feel invincible. Bring it on, we can get through anything.

On day eight, the rain stops although the heat is agonizingly relentless. At least now our basin is overflowing, and with all that rainfall, there are sure to be countless natural water reservoirs in the garden. I can see bright red and purple fruit weighing down the brambles nearby. It makes my stomach growl.

I walk over with the wooden bowl Jake widdled from the knot of a freshly fallen tree limb, intent on eating my fill and then loading up the bowl for Jake. The water glistens off every surface in the full sun, the waterlogged ground squishy under my feet. I reach the berry patch but stop dead in my tracks.

Tiny, sickly, cream-colored worms jut in and out of the red berries, chewing through fruity flesh as far as the eye can see. Spider mites devour leaves, green foliage there one minute, gone the next. Like an army of invaders in formation, intent on destroying everything in their path. I take a step back feeling the sick coming to the surface.

I turn back to our little encampment and watch in horror as a funnel cloud of gnats descends on Achilles and mosquitos attack in swarms so thick they look like miniature tornados sweeping across the land. I scream and stomp at the same time when I feel belligerent red ants crawling all over my feet.

I look down and bellow again when I notice the ground is animated with a million crawling insects. Ticks land on my shift, in my hair. Beetles scuttle between branches, some taking flight, propelled by two sets of wings. Bugs everywhere; hairy, shiny, striped, plain, bright, dull, some as big as my thumb, others no bigger than a speck.

"Jake, Jake!" my voice is wild. "Jake, what's happening? Where are they coming from? Why?"

Jake is standing on a crooked root, not nearly as disturbed by this madness as me. He is surveying the landscape.

"This is what happens when nature is out of balance Evey. Too much heat, too much rain, it's not natural. Too much growth, too fast. A perfect storm."

He trails off. He doesn't have to spell it out for me. All those lessons in unintended consequences. All the possible repercussions of destroying the equilibrium. The ancient experiences with unpredictable weather patterns, unstable geological systems, unreliable food supply.

And had they continued, an uninhabitable earth. Who would have guessed that their ultimate downfall might have been this? An uncontrollable, uncontainable infestation. Death by pestilence.

Chapter 13

'I beg you take courage; the brave soul can mend even disaster.'
—Catherine the Great, Last Empress of Russia

It rains just enough to keep the thirst at bay. It seems every time the reservoir approaches empty, the skies open up. Achilles is somewhat protected from the constant barrage of insects with his thick coat, but the incessant heat must be excruciating for him. He doesn't complain, but I worry. He was made for ice and cold, this can't be good for him.

I know it's not good for us. I watch Jake as he reinforces the roof between the giant roots of our makeshift shelter. We are in for another drenching. We will have to re-apply the mud after this rain, it is the only way to keep from going mad.

We look savage, our hair slicked back, our skin caked with layers of dirt. The creepy crawlies are multiplying by the minute. I am reduced to celebrating each time a silky spider web traps a new flying bug, one less to worry about.

The woodland creatures are suffering too. We hear them thrashing through the forest. When we catch sight of them, they are filthy, using the same strategy we are for a reprieve from the biting insects.

Yesterday, I found Jake standing with his back to our encampment, unmoving except for his hands, balling in and out of fists. My heart leapt into my throat when I didn't see Achilles. When I approached, I am loathe to admit, I was relieved to find him poised over a red fox, opaque eyes staring up at Jake, pleading for mercy.

Thick, cracked skin on ears and nose, patches of a once lush coat replaced with painful scales, emaciation that turned my stomach. Mange. Like every other insect in the animal kingdom, the cancerous mites that infect indiscriminately will be thriving, destroying every fur-bearing creature in their path.

I don't know how much longer we can survive this heat. Where is it even coming from? It feels like we are sitting on the mouth of another volcano, hidden under our feet. I sigh, it is pointless to speculate, I might as well be doing something helpful.

Jake is digging a hole near the fox we found yesterday, intent on offering it a dignified end. He feels responsible for every living thing in the garden. His pain is tangible, rolling off of him like water. I don't speak but walk over and kneel beside him, start pulling weeds and moving stones that will become a grave site.

I know there will be so many more and we won't be able to bury them all, but here, today, this one act symbolizes the respect we have for every living creature.

The scene renews my anxiety about Achilles, but then, according to legend, he is the Waheela, somehow, he's survived a thousand years. I have to trust that he will be protected. The wolf sits patiently a short distance off, smart enough to stay away from the diseased carcass, his subdued demeanor suggesting he shares in our sorrow.

Jake is careful not to touch the remains, using the butt end of a thick branch to push the animal into the hole. I witness his transcendence as he offers his blessing and grants the spirit permission to move on. Not with pride, but not with humility either.

Gone is the adorably self-deprecating boy with the easy smile. I realize Jake was always destined to be here. I suddenly feel unworthy of this man, molded as if by the hands of the Maker himself. Talk about a hard act to follow.

And on cue, he senses my diffidence, wraps an impressive bicep around my shoulder and tugs me close, kissing the top of my head. I wrap my arms around his equally impressive torso, and we stand sandwiched together for a long, silent moment. Our current predicament seems somehow less significant, his strength replenishing my faith. We can survive this.

Dinner time is becoming tedious. We have to scrutinize every nut, every berry, every root, before adding it to our already limited menu. The thought of chomping down on a worm or larvae makes my skin crawl.

Jake insists we force ourselves to secure enough calories no matter how long it takes. We cannot afford to become enfeebled by malnourishment even though I would rather trade less mealtime for more sleep time.

I feel a shift in the environment as the days wear on. The infinite assortment of pests; aphids, moths, gnats, mosquitos, fleas, ticks, ants, beetles…I think their numbers might actually be dwindling. We don't scratch or swat at them nearly as much as we have been.

Achilles is finally able to settle without constantly pawing at his ears or twitching uncontrollably. But in their stead, the bees arrive. I've never paid them much mind, a bee is a bee is a bee. Now that I watch them dance amidst the petal soft raindrops, I truly see them for the first time. I am fascinated by the diversity.

A profusion of colors and sizes, some hairy, some smooth, shiny, dull, plain, striped. They don't attack, in fact, I might be imagining it, but it's as though they lord over all the other insects in the garden and are keeping them at bay for us.

I've grown so accustomed to the urtication; the weals spot my body like a leopard print. I don't know what to do with my hands; they finally settle as the incessant itching subsides. I sit blissfully motionless as my skin begins to absorb the welts one by one.

I want nothing more than to lie down and close my eyes, allowing my nerve endings to wallow in the respite. Jake and Achilles have the same idea, both already resting peacefully under an overhang, the branch serving as a giant umbrella. I am about to join them, give in to the fatigue, when the bees close in and swarm me. Not stinging, not even touching, but encircling my head. Like a crown.

"Juh, Juh, Jake," my voice quivers.

I don't know if I've projected enough to wake him. His hands are folded under his head, legs crossed comfortably over one another. Achilles lays by his side, the sound of their light snoring and the pitter-patter of raindrops drowned out by the whirring of the bees as they go round and round, never breaking formation.

Achilles' lip peels back in a snarl and he jumps to his feet, Jake lurches a second later with a look of bewilderment, his brain scrambling with the abrupt transition.

"Uhm, over here?" I say self-consciously, my lips moving, but careful to keep my head very, very still.

"Evey!" Jake swallows the space between us in four giant steps but leaves a healthy gap, eyeing the mob of bees racing around my head.

He looks mortified.

"Right?" I jest. "I mean, do I look like a sunflower to you?"

"Very funny, Evey. What if, I mean, maybe you should try to move?"

My eyes go wide, and he adds a graceless, "Slowly?"

Sure. What's the worst that can happen? A few hundred bee stings to the side of the face? Walk in the park. I don't say this out loud, he is only trying to help. Then again, they could have stung me to death by now, yet they abstain. And it's not like I can sit here in suspended animation forever.

Okay then.

If I can only get my limbs to cooperate. It takes three tries for my paralyzed motor functioning to respond. The bees shift with my movements, adjusting their flight pattern to maintain the same trajectory around my head as I rise and take two steps forward. Another two steps, same effect.

Like the moth to a flame, *close* is enough for them. I turn to my left. Something changes. They accelerate, the buzzing intensifies, as though they are panicking. I reverse the turn. The frantic pace of their beating wings and what feels to me like a state of agitation recedes immediately.

Jake is watching with his mouth hanging half open, Achilles sitting at his feet, head tilted to one side, no longer showing any signs of distress. This has to be a good sign. I look at the wolf as I take two more steps toward them, his tail twitches, ears tweak, but there is no aggression in his body language.

The bees follow, with no hint of protestation. It's as if they are communicating with me. Another step, I test my theory and turn left again to the same intense reaction, a definite objection.

Okay, not left then. As we continue this dance-step, check, advance, retreat, step, check—I have to wonder. Why me? This is Jake's domain, he is the shepherd, the champion. Shouldn't they be connecting with him?

Jake and Achilles follow at a safe distance while this living wreath moves me along, to where I have no idea. Their restraint is astonishing, not one upsets the delicate configuration.

We walk out of our clearing, through the trees and undergrowth until we reach a cave carved into the landscape. Large, grey rock of a type I don't recognize, almost flimsy-looking, protrudes from the earth, ostensibly out of nowhere. It looks so out of place.

A new energy emanates from the bees as they direct me toward the opening of this strange grotto. I glance back at Achilles, looking for his counsel. He seems at ease. Jake, on the other hand, is ghostly pale, with an angst the wolf clearly does not share. I take my cue from the Waheela.

As I pass the threshold, I lay my hand on the face of the rock to steady myself. It feels like parchment paper, a greasy texture that gives under my weight. I pull my hand back instantly at the unexpected sensation.

My eyes adjust to the waning light and I register a geometrical pattern, a mathematical precision, to this cave. It takes me a minute, I have to adjust my perspective, zoom out, my eyes working like the aperture of a camera lens. Comprehension hits me like a smack in the face.

Repeating six-sided cells surround me, over and over and over. Hexagons. A surge of panic coats my skin with a million tiny pinpricks while my heart picks up a gallop. This is no cave. I am in the hive.

The moment I try to turn back, the bees dissuade me with a flash of anger marked by a feverish velocity, tightening the sphere around my face to emphasize their displeasure. Achilles whimpers behind me.

"Evey," Jake speaks for the first time since we entered this catacomb. "We are right here with you. It looks as though we have to see this through."

"Yup. Got it."

At least he said *we*.

I keep moving forward through this endless honeycomb on leaden legs. We reach what I surmise is the center of the hive as the walls and ceiling give way to an expansive cavity. Shafts of light filter in from tunnels extending to the surface like skylights, creating a warmth to the space that I would not have thought possible.

As my eyes rove, the circlet of bees descends as one, then land as one, on the hard packed floor of the hive. The flickers of movement from worker bees in the hexagonal chambers all around me suddenly stops altogether, no more buzz of beating wings, not even the twitch of antennae, they are so still I think they may have all perished.

Jake and Achilles tiptoe to my side and then the great wolf drops flat on the floor, ears pressed against his head, tail straight out and unmoving. A display of total submission. Jake and I exchange a glance, his raised brow tells me he doesn't understand what is happening any more than I do.

Something is coming from the opposite end of the cavern; it is so stagnant in here I can feel the vibration before I see anything. But when I do, see it, a rush of adrenaline courses through my body like an erupting geyser. I feel Jake stiffen beside me, Achilles tips his snout even closer to the floor.

It, no, she, somehow, I am certain of this, hovers on two sets of iridescent wings so large, I can feel wind on my face. The forewings sparkle in the streamers of light, the smaller hindwings shimmer like satin.

Her head and thorax are covered with a luxurious fur coat in shades of milky yellow and fiery orange with hints of bronze and gold. Her abdomen is long and slender, sleek in a way the other bees are not.

She lands directly in front of me, her height matching my own as she balances herself on a menacing barbed stinger protruding from the end of her belly, stabilized by powerful hindlegs and thickly cushioned back feet. I see myself reflected a million times over in her enormous, depthless compound eyes, each facet an inescapable mirror.

My throat clears of its own volition when I notice she is looking at me with three more eyes, the ocelli, smaller, simple eyes triangulated just above two long articulating tentacles sprouting from a forehead covered in gossamer fur. She is so close, the mandibles jutting from her lower jaw like razor-sharp claws brush my chin when she extends them outward. She reaches out with a single antenna, and rubs it along my cheek, soft as a caress.

I don't move. I don't even blink. She is somehow beautiful, despite being utterly horrifying at the same time. I don't look away; I don't bow my head. She is truly a queen.

A voice like liquid silver fills the air, pouring from every cell in the honeycomb. A voice that cannot, will not, be ignored, dripping with majesty.

"No Everett Steele. We are not queens. We are queens of queens. Just as you are sovereign of your kind, I am the supreme ruler of my kind. And we two, answer to the *One*. I have been summoned to hold counsel with you. Empress to empress."

Come again? Did that just happen in my head? I see Jake in my periphery and judging by the look on his face that would be a negative. He heard it too. Me? Empress? That's ludicrous. I am no queen of anything.

"But you are. And you will be. You are destined to become the mother of mothers. Like me."

Okay, she's actually reading my mind. I look askance at Jake who is impossibly white as the implications of the Empress's message register. Holy spoiler alert.

She looks down at the legion of bees that escorted us here.

"My drones have done well. They will be rewarded."

She salutes her minions by extending a middle leg, her version of a pat on the head for a job well done.

Drones. All males. I was never in any danger of being stung. I glance down at her soldiers, standing at attention, awaiting her next command. Total subservience.

With the elegance of a butterfly, she floats to Jake and Achilles, standing a few feet to my left.

"The Chosen One, this I expected, but—"

She is way more interested in Achilles.

"Waheela."

Achilles rises slowly to a sitting position. He bows his head. And then to my surprise, she tips hers to him, equals professing mutual respect.

"It seems you now have two conduits to the *One*. And two blessings. The Waheela blesses you with his protection, and in turn, your preservation."

She waits as if I am supposed to say something.

"Uh, yes, yes, he has helped in so many ways I've lost count. We wouldn't be standing here without him."

"Indeed."

Two beats of her magnificent wings and she is right back in front of me, those unnerving eyes assessing me once again.

"And you are bonded with yet another."

Again, she pauses, watching.

Images of my family flash in my mind. I feel a sharp pang of guilt. Since I arrived in the garden, there has not been a moment to properly reflect on what my decision has cost my parents, my brother, my grandmother. The pain I must have caused them. It was an impossible choice, but I have to believe I made the right one. She interrupts my self-torment.

"No, I am referring to your bond with the other."

Jake shifts beside me. Clearly this is news to him. But I don't know who she is talking about.

"You do, Everett Steele."

It is downright disturbing that my every thought is psychoanalyzed and broadcasted through this matrix of cells. I stomp on this thought lest she expose this too. I focus instead on the other.

Like a phantasmagoria, he materializes in every chamber, the hive projecting an execrable image that I cannot evade. I gasp audibly at his grotesque disfigurement, the engorgement of his face and neck, the hematomas spotting him everywhere, rendering him inhuman, making him look more like a poorly stuffed scarecrow.

Purplish bruising interspersed between the pools of blood, mucus dribbling from horrendously swollen lips, his hair matted with sweat, toxic-looking yellow-brown smears defiling his entire form.

Jake stares. Achilles whimpers. The Empress is solemn.

Tears blur my vision, a small mercy. His name slips from my lips, unbidden.

"Pedro."

Chapter 14

'Though one may be overpowered, two can defend themselves. A cord of three strands is not quickly broken.'

—Ecclesiastes 4:12 (NIV)

The Empress lets me process a moment, recognizing the anguish that accompanies the shock that must be written all over my face. When she finally speaks, her tone is subdued.

"My colony was deceived. Baited. Of course, I will punish them if that is your will."

No apology, but the conciliation is a fair consolation.

Jake shares his thoughts for the first time since we encountered the Empress.

"I don't know this, Pedro, but this situation definitely has the stink of Draeger all over it."

"Pedro," I repeat in a whisper. "Jake, Pedro is immune, like we are. Were."

The Empress fills in the gaps.

"Yes, the boy is the third. You are not complete without him. Birth, life, death. Body, mind, spirit. Wisdom, knowledge, understanding."

Jake addresses me directly now.

"You, know him, Evey?"

"We've met. We were here, together, last year. And then…remember when Draeger had Mom? And the tetra was, well, sort of crushing the life out of me?"

Achilles lets out a low growl. I gather he comprehends what I've just revealed. Jake reaches down and soothes him with a gentle touch.

"Well, Pedro was there too. He stopped the tetra from destroying the Biodome."

"Whoa. Evey, you never told me about this," Jake looks confused.

"Geez, Jake, give a girl a break. Been a little busy?"

The Empress is looking from me to Jake and back. If I didn't know better, I'd say she's amused.

"Wait. He's been here. Like, here?"

"Yes, at the tree. There was a, a wet fleece, it was out back, behind the tree."

I can see the wheels turning in Jake's mind. His eyes are squinty, he's nodding almost imperceptibly. Then his head snaps up.

"Wait! I didn't do that. I found it at my doorstep, it was a vulture or a raptor or something."

"It's okay Jake, now is not the time."

I glance at the Empress.

He nods and changes the subject.

"Do you know what this means Evey?"

Ugh, nope, can't say I do.

"He can cross over! Just like you did!"

I look at the Empress, who has been silent, observing our exchange. Her lyrical voice echoes anew in the chambers.

"The Chosen One is correct. In his current state, the boy will need your help to find his way, but it can be done."

"But what about his body? I was in a health promotion facility, under supervision, cared for while I was here. What will happen to him?"

She considers a moment.

"If you will permit, my colony will protect his human form from harm."

I take it all in. I have to save him; I have to try.

"Okay. What do we do?"

It feels like pushing against an elastic membrane, I can't break through, but I can stretch it. The mental exertion of forcing my way through dimensions is wreaking havoc on me physically, my heart is racing, every nerve ending thrumming, my muscles cramping with the buildup of lactic acid.

I've only met Pedro twice in my life, but the Empress is right. There is a deep connection that I cannot define, a feeling, a bond, a kinship. It has to be enough. I can't let him die.

Through a curtain of static, like an untuned radio, I hear the Empress.

"No. It must be her."

And then Jake.

"It's hurting her. Let me help her." He sounds fraught with anxiety.

"She is stronger than you think. She will persevere. Have faith."

I don't need this distraction. It is taking every fiber of my being to infiltrate this renitent veil. Have faith, have faith, have faith…The words resonate all around me on a phantom wind.

The same words Pedro said to me when we were trapped in the Biodome. When hope was abandoning me. I let him take my hands and his faith filled me. And we made it.

I stop my assault. Let it all melt away and fall to my knees. My head drops, in equal parts supplication and fatigue. I can't *shove* my way through. *Have faith*, I tell myself.

When I open my eyes, I am kneeling at Pedro's side. His breathing is dangerously shallow and guttural. But alive. I brush my fingers across his disfigured brow, the blistering fever sticks to my hand. I bring my lips close to his ear with an urgent whisper.

"Pedro, Pedro. Please."

Nothing.

"Pedro, it's Everett. Remember your *senhora*?"

He stirs, accompanied by a pained moaning sound. One eye opens to a slit, the other a calamity of inflammation that's rendered it inoperable.

"Don't try to talk," I hush him. "I can take you away from here, I can take you to a safe place, a place where I can help you."

His one eye is tracking me, his faculties intact.

"Pedro, I can take you home with me, but I can't promise I can bring you back. I don't know the rules, exactly."

His eye opens wider, questioning.

I spot Draeger in the distance, sauntering casually up the walkway toward this little compound. Jake was right, this is all his doing.

"Pedro, I don't have time to explain. We have to go. Now. I need a signal."

A meagre nod, so slight I almost miss it. But I don't. And it's all I need.

Draeger rolls the gold-tipped pen through his fingers with the dexterity of a maestro. It is a habit he has developed when deep in thought.

No, it was not by my hand, I merely locked the gate.

I am not responsible for the behavior of creatures created by the Other's own hand. I did not put them here.

And no, my actions were not borne of a desire for petty vengeance.

I am certain the boy was here for Everett Steele, there is no such thing as coincidence. I was justified.

He'd been monitoring Pedro's movements for days. His suspicions were confirmed when the willful agent headed straight for the equine complex upon his arrival and substantiated beyond doubt, as he'd managed the brief convergence.

When he passed the boy on the pathway, he'd held the connection long enough to intuit that the boy was holding on to something so compelling that it frightened him to his very core. Simple observation told Draeger the boy's briefcase contained this earth-shattering revelation.

He'd conducted his impromptu apiary agents' meeting under the guise of some new safety measures he wanted implemented, excused the team for the remainder of the day, and adopting a leisurely pace, made his way back to check on his handiwork.

The gruesome scene takes him aback. He has witnessed much carnage over the centuries, countless examples of the toll of man-made conflict on the human body. But this. Even for him, the devastation is shocking. It is eerily quiet now, the legion of destroyers returned to their lair.

What remains is the husk of a boy. Bloated beyond recognition. Mottled skin, red and purple. Black and blue. Wavy hair matted with greasy sweat. A shallow wheeze emanates between deformed lips. Sticky mustardy yellow daubs cover the boy like a disease. Excrement, Draeger realizes with disgust.

He watches the boy for a long minute, half expecting him to expire right in front of him. Knowing his soul is untouchable, that he belongs to the Other. No point pining for something you can never have.

He reaches for the briefcase lying a short distance from the prone form. As he retreats, he looks back one last time, almost admiring the boys' will to live. There is no doubt Pedro Ramón beat the world record.

He is almost at the gate when his curiosity gets the better of him. Perhaps the boy holds more information. He glances at the briefcase in his hand. Will this reveal all? Or is there more to be learned? This is his last chance; the boy will be found soon enough. It will only take a minute, two at most, just a touch.

Draeger turns back. The thought of soiling his hands on the boy is distasteful but decidedly worth the repugnance. A dozen steps and he halts abruptly, his hands flying to his face in a truly rare instance of being taken off guard. He can just make out Pedro, unmoving but for the pitiable rise and fall of his chest as the boy labors to breathe, his line of sight badly obscured by a wall of bees blocking his path.

He scours the makeshift camp for clues. He has only been gone a half hour, three quarters at most. He'd been inspired by the boy's ire at the demise of a pathetic *Canidae*, his contemptible doggedness at seeing to a dignified burial for the lowly creature.

In fact, He'd so delighted in demoralizing the lad that He decided to unleash his golem on an unsuspecting bevy of white-tailed deer languishing just north of their settlement, slaughtering indiscriminately. If the boy was crestfallen over a mangy fox, He was jubilant at the thought of the boys' impending misery when they inevitably uncovered this immortalized Bambi and his family.

A valuable lesson in war; don't underestimate the importance of breaking the spirit of your enemy. It was worth the cost, his strength depleted for just a short time.

He positioned the golem just out of site of the bloodbath, well-hidden behind a copse of thick saplings and young conifers and crept back to this now empty lot. They must have gone in search of nutriment.

He capitalizes on the unexpected solitude to replenish himself, soaking in the resonant heat of his scorched earth. Just as his slender body begins to numb, sleep tickling the edges of his mind, his honed tactile senses register a sudden, rhythmic quivering.

He has grown adept at deciphering acoustic waves but this, this is alien. Not water, or seismic activity, much too panoptic to be man-made. Not without a focal point though. He lifts his snout, scenting the air with his primitive lingual organ. There, up ahead, to his right.

Fully alert now, He edges his way toward ground zero, adopting a slow, calculated approach. Sixty feet into his foray, the garden explodes with blinding white light. He shields his eyes with opaque scales, filtering the intensity of the blast.

The garden disappears and He falls into nothingness. Flailing, his elongated tail whipping in the wind, He tries to right himself. With a heavy thump, He hits the ground, choking on a spasm as his lungs slap the Earth.

Then nothing but quiet. The garden re-materializes as if passing through a heavy fog. He lies still, holding his breath. His fury spills over, red coloring his golden eyes. There can be but one explanation. Divine interference. The Other.

In two blinks she's gone. Jake reaches for the emptiness where she stood seconds ago. Achilles sniffs at the air but makes no move to advance. Jake stares haplessly at the Empress, processing a jumble of emotions, none of them pleasant. The regal queen slants those hypnotic eyes, Jake can sense her disapproval.

"You doubt your queen, Chosen One."

A statement, not a question. It rattles him.

He snorts out an exasperated breath and gathers his wits about him. Not time to fall apart.

"No. I never doubt Evey. Worry, fret, stress, yes. But never doubt."

This seems to placate the Empress. Her voice softens.

"Very well. Let me put your mind at ease. Your queen will return to you unscathed."

Just as the echo of her message fades into the catacombs, Jake is blown backwards by a concentrated wave of energy so intense it distorts the hive. Stumbling but not losing his footing entirely, he reaches for Achilles, reassuring the wolf with a firm hand on the animal's head.

The Empress does not appear to be fazed whatsoever. She hovers a moment, easily dissipating the impact of the blast and then sets herself back down gracefully. As if she were expecting it.

On the heels of the sonic detonation, Jake is momentarily blinded by an achromatic glow that bleaches the entire landscape. The hive, the Empress, her bees, all rendered white. The wolf all but disappears at his side, white on white. Jake is disoriented by a blizzard of spots, his shocked retina responding to the overstimulation.

When the field of floaters dissolve and color slowly returns to the garden, he blinks twice and scrunches his face up. When he opens his eyes, she is standing there, hand-in-hand, with a perfect stranger.

He looks from Everett to the tanned and toned male at her side, then to the Empress, and finally, a questioning glance at Achilles. The wolf confirms that this is not a figment, he is clearly sizing him up. Everett is the first to break the uncomfortable silence.

"Jake, this is Pedro, Pedro, meet Jake."

Jake stares at their clasped hands. Everett follows his line of sight and relinquishes the intimate union.

Of all the things to focus on right now, Jake rebukes himself.

"So, Pedro, it's uhm, nice to make your acquaintance."

Jake cringes at his own watery introduction.

"*Senhor* Jake," his name comes out as *Jacques* in Pedro's dialect, lending the boy an air of sophistication juxtaposed with a childlike innocence that makes him instantly likeable.

Trying to find a better icebreaker, Everett saves him by interjecting.

"What happened to you Pedro? What are you doing in the northwest quadrant? No scratch that, what are you doing at Midwest AW? You haven't carried your injuries over. Are you, okay?" she peppers him with questions.

Pedro has a befuddled look about him like he's trying to inventory her queries.

"The bees," he starts, his eyes going impossibly wide when the Empress sidles in from the shadows.

A look of abject terror washes over his handsome features, his face draining of all color. Everett stops him from backing up with a hand on his shoulder.

"It's okay, Pedro, this is the Empress. She won't hurt you, she's on our side."

Pedro's pallor remains dull as dead leaves as he studies the prodigious Hymenoptera. Jake can almost see the wheels turning as the boy's horror morphs into scientific curiosity. Pedro resumes talking, never taking his eyes off the Empress.

"The bees," he says again, this time without any disparagement. "They were, provoked."

The Empress seems mollified by Pedro's explanation and change in tone, her version of events now corroborated. Pedro continues to choose his words carefully.

"I was locked in the ground nest compound when they were disturbed. It was only, ah, *naturau*, what is the word, *si*, 'natural' that they would attack."

The Empress is almost nodding her approval.

"But, Pedro, why were you there in the first place?"

Everett sounds a tad impatient.

He peels his eyes away from the Empress and looks directly at Everett.

"I was looking for you, *senhora*."

Jake's emotions take a nosedive. Could it be that Everett was moving on? Did he drag her away from a newfound romance? He looks between Everett and Pedro, sensing the connection. Is this the part where his heart gets ripped out? He'd just assumed when she came back…He holds his breath. Everett's response is anything but romantic.

"Me? Why?"

Jake's spirits are instantly uplifted. Maybe he's reading the situation all wrong.

"I have discovered new information, *senhora*," Pedro replies. "I did not know who else to trust. You and I, *senhora*, we have both seen things, done things, that no one else would understand. I had to find you. We have been here before, *si*?"

Everett blanches slightly.

"Uh, ya, this is the same place, Pedro. Except, well, except, I kind of live here now. Like permanently."

Pedro's head swivels between Jake and Everett. His mouth is opening and closing, but nothing is coming out.

"I know. It's a lot." Everett tries to soothe him.

"*Senhora*, you are trapped here?"

"No, not exactly. I chose to come. Just like Jake chose to come. We can't go back."

Pedro's warm skin takes on a greenish olive tone.

"Does this mean, I, too, cannot go back? I cannot go home?"

Everett looks at the Empress as if she has the right answer. When she offers nothing, Everett winces.

"I don't know, Pedro. I'm not sure. I do know that you would have died in that apiary compound. The Empress saved you."

The Empress counters Everett's statement. Pedro jumps as her velvety voice is transmitted throughout the hive.

"I was alerted to my colony's grave error. However, Everett Steele has overstated my role in your extrication. Nevertheless, my children will protect your earthly form while you are with us."

She pauses as if debating what to say.

"And to your question. The Master is not a deceiver. Your free will is intact."

Jake can see that Pedro is in awe of the majestic insect. He tilts his head observing the bee from different angles. Is he actually counting the lens of her compound eye? Jake clears his throat to focus his attention to the present. The Empress appears amused.

"*Si, desculpa Imperatriz.* I have lost my manners."

Everett cuts in.

"Well, that's good news now, isn't it? So now that we've got that sorted out, why don't you fill us in on this new information?"

Pedro begins by shaking his head vigorously, his attention split in ten different directions at once. He starts, stops, then starts again, as if he can't quite remember how to use his tongue.

"Pedro. Spill."

Everett plasters on a fake frown.

Pedro takes a deep breath.

"I found a file on Dr. Draeger. I don't think it was ever intended to be found, you see. My *professora*, Dr. Castillo," he makes the sign of the cross, "discovered Draeger's true paternity."

"Oh kay," Everett stretches out the acknowledgement.

"Is that such a big deal? I mean, we all know he's bad news, but what does his father have to do with it?"

Jake is thinking the same thing.

"You don't understand. Vladimir Draeger is…he is the son of Abaddon," Pedro declares.

Say who? Jake is lost, but Everett's face has gone ghastly pale. What is he missing?

"The six and one," she whispers.

The Empress is so still that Jake has to double-check that she hasn't turned to stone.

"The power in a name…not *who* you are, but *what* you are." Everett shudders.

"Hold on," Jake is mildly annoyed now. "I know, I've been gone a while now, but would someone please let me in on the punch line please?"

Everett turns her wild blue eyes to Jake, her expression lost, hopeless, timorous, all at once.

"Jake, the tetra. The tetra is Abaddon. Draeger is the son of the Destroyer."

Jake laughs.

"Ha! I always knew Draeger was a snake!"

Neither Everett nor Pedro laughs along with his joke. Wait, they're serious?

"*Nao*," Pedro says very slowly. "And the great dragon was thrown down, the serpent of old who is called the devil and Satan, who deceives the whole world; he was thrown down to the earth, and his angels were thrown down with him," he recites from the Book of Revelation.

Jake tries to follow, looking at Everett for help. She shakes her head.

"Don't bother," she advises. "Give him a minute, it always makes sense. Eventually."

Pedro explains, "All of them, thrown down. One destined to become ruler of the Abyss. Cursed to walk the Earth in reptilian form."

Pedro eyes Jake.

"Dr. Draeger is no snake. He is an angel."

Nope, still not making sense to Jake. Everett gives him a look that says *patience*.

"He is a son of the Fallen. And yet, he roams the Earth as a man. That should not be possible. Unless—"

Pedro scratches at his temple. A minute goes by before he finishes his thought.

"His *mãe*. *Si! Si!* Draeger is half-human, his mother was mortal. His father is…That is how he survived. It all makes sense now."

Pedro rubs absentmindedly at his right arm.

Jake knits his brow, and Everett makes a squinty face.

"What? I did say, *eventually*," she shrugs.

Pedro rubs his chin, still thinking out loud, still marching to his own drummer.

"We rid the Biodome of Abaddon, but we certainly did not destroy him. He is, he has to be, somewhere! But where? *Arco de rabeca!*"

Fiddlestick is Pedro's version of a curse word.

"Well, that's easy," Everett quips.

Pedro gives her a most perplexed look.

"Why didn't you just ask that in the first place? He's right here."

Pedro stops ranting, projecting that same quizzical stare.

"You are sure, *senhora*?"

Jake approaches and proffers his left hand. Two prominent, hypertrophic puncture wounds in the early stages of healing stand out on his pink flesh like a beacon.

"Ya, pretty sure," is all he says.

Chapter 15

'Constant misfortune brings this one blessing: to whom it always assails, it eventually fortifies.'

—Lucius Annaeus Seneca (c. 1 BCE–CE 65)

Pedro examines the scars on Jake's hand while Everett explains that their little exorcism from the Biodome landed the tetra right back here, in the Beginning. And so, she had to come back for Jake, to protect him, despite what it must have done to her family. Pedro doesn't meet her eyes, the sorrow at the mentions her mother, father, and brother colors her words.

Everett explains that she thought she was too late but, with the help of the enormous *lobo branco* now watching his every move, they neutralized the venom and well, Jake survived.

Pedro peers at the great wolf out of the corner of his eye, noticing that Jake treats the animal more like a lap dog than the great beast he is, tugging at his fur and making funny faces at him. Meanwhile 'Achilles' makes Pedro all kinds of nervous.

"But, but, why?" Pedro stammers. "Why is he returned *here*? Why not return somewhere in the Biodome and wreak havoc from there?"

The sleek, melodious voice of the Empress fills the chamber in response.

"He needs to destroy the Beginning so there can be no second chance for mankind. Without the Chosen One, man will remain forever tarnished and exploitable. He is, as you humans like to say, playing the long game."

"I guess that fits with his M.O," Jake states simply.

"But I mean, he could have just finished me off in the Biodome, could have saved himself all the trouble of chasing me across dimensions."

Pedro is confused. Everett proceeds to explain the backstory, cliff notes version, but enough to fill his boots with a combination of fascination and desolation. The genetic hack is especially remarkable to his mind. He stands, slack-jawed, soaking it all in.

"I know," Jake pipes up, "it's a lot. And I lived it."

"So, now what?" Everett throws her hands up, clearly vexed by the situation.

"It seems like we just keep going around and around in this cat-and-mouse game."

In response, the Empress addresses Pedro.

"Well, young one? Have you decided? Your will is your own, you can wash your hands of this and return if you wish."

Pedro doesn't even hesitate, shaking his head, his teeth clenched. He picks up on Everett's cat-and-mouse idiom, his intentions clear in the role reversal.

"Sharpen your claws *gatinha* (kitty). This is *our* gift, *our* Beginning."

He bows deferentially toward Jake, "Let's catch us a mouse."

Frustrated at this form's limitation with airborne sound, He strains to decipher the conversation that grows louder as the pair approaches, that vexatious mutt in tow.

The boy's tenor is muffled to his inferior inner ear, but his animation is nonetheless evident.

"I knew it! I knew it was Draeger. It reeks of that despot!"

And the gratingly angelic rejoinder of the female.

"You were right, Jake, you called it."

In the crepuscular light, he can only make out their outlines approaching from the west. He freezes when an unidentified voice projects from the growing darkness.

"*Si, Senhor*, I believe Dr. Draeger was seeking vengeance for my attempt on his life," Pedro refers to his earlier recounting of the harrowing standoff.

What is this now? His third is here? This is the audacious mortal who dared enter my domain. Who dared attack my son?

He is somewhat surprised at the short-sightedness of the Other's play. With all three of them here in the garden, the Biodome is fully exposed. Nothing left but blemished souls; Vladimir will be completely unopposed. His sons' hold on power is all but assured now.

With that burden lifted, now He can focus on destroying the Other's contingency plan. He almost relishes the challenge. First, He will collect more intel. He waits patiently, observes, listens.

After the three arrive back at the encampment, the Chosen One effortlessly kindles a flame and before long, an assortment of roots and leaves are placed over the flames. The new one seems in his element in the forest, not in the least distressed by the lack of amenities.

Moreover, there appears to be a prolific *anthophila* population swarming about the camp, creating a most effective deterrence against his legion of vermin. They no longer seem bothered by his pestilence. His disconcertment grows by the minute.

The Chosen One takes the female by the hand and leads her to a small clearing a short distance from the camp.

"Evey, are you upset? I mean, I so did not see that coming either."

He clambers a little closer through the forest debris, curious about this conversation that seems to require discretion.

"No Jake, well, maybe, I don't know!"

The female runs her hands through her long hair, fidgeting from foot to foot.

"Since I've been back, we've jumped from crisis to crisis. We haven't even explored, us. I mean, how could we, with all, this."

She extends her arms out as if to emphasize her point.

"It's not that I haven't wanted to, Ev."

He brushes a thumb against her cheekbone.

"The Empress didn't say anything about, like, timelines, or anything."

The Empress? What is 'she' doing here? Why would He summon her? This has nothing to do with her or her kind. Well, it certainly explains the surfeit of humblebees.

"I know, it's my own fault. I should never have asked her about her blessing. I should have just been grateful for Achilles and his protection and kept my mouth shut."

She did not...He seethes.

The boy's lips are curved into an irrepressible smile.

"Well, at least we don't have to worry about *that*, if, and when the time comes. I mean, how many people can say their union is sanctified by the Goddess of Fertility?"

She did.

Maureen Domanso lingers in the hallway outside the boy's room. Now that his vitals are stabilized, the last of the stingers removed, his thready breath growing stronger and deeper, her thoughts drift to the strange circumstances surrounding this calamity. The apiary agents reported finding the boy this morning inside the ground nest enclosure.

Genevieve Levine, the apiary lead, a mild-mannered and soft-spoken woman in her early 40s, explains that the education and research agent from the Southwest Biodome is part of a new joint initiative in apitherapy development. She is unaware of who, if anyone, escorted the visiting agent.

She is baffled as to how he accessed the compound, emphasizing that it is under lock and key. Given its occupants, the security measures are for everyone's protection.

Dr. Levine looks at her three team members in turn, all bug-eyed and shaking their heads defensively, genuinely oblivious. Maureen looks skeptically at the four agents.

"What were you all doing that was so engrossing that you missed a complete stranger sauntering into your program and accessing your most dangerous research site, without the proper equipment no less?"

There is something missing here, the story is not adding up.

"Ms. Domanso, I was only following orders. I was told to bring the team to main administration for a meeting that lasted all afternoon yesterday." Dr. Levine is circumspect.

"I see," Maureen processes this new information.

"And who called this meeting?" Her suspicion is not quite quashed.

"Dr. Draeger himself."

Levine is dripping with trepidation at the mention of his name.

Now it's quashed. Completely.

"Dr. Levine, you are excused. My apologies for the interrogation. It was necessary, given the exigent circumstances."

The tension in the corridor evaporates with the pardon, the apiary agents lined up against the wall almost slumping in relief.

"Of course."

Dr. Levine nods politely to Maureen and ushers her agents down the hallway and out the back door.

Maureen enters the ailing agent's room and puts her hands in the pockets of her slim-fitting trousers as she approaches the bed. She narrows her eyes as she watches the sleeping boy and half-mumbles.

"First Jacob, then Everett, and now, you."

Sandra Steele is annoyed. She yanks on the hem of her navy skirt a little too forcefully and shoves her feet into stylish wedge heels, her go-to wardrobe staple. Maureen Domanso has a lot of nerve demanding an audience. Sandra definitely lost her cool during their last confrontation, she has to keep her wits about her today.

No doubt Draeger's second in command wants to assess whether she is still committed to challenging that monster's authority. Which she most certainly is, but it is still early days.

Definitely a little premature, she thinks, but she can't refuse the meeting. She owes the woman that much. An apology might be a stretch. Is she truly sorry for striking her? The woman did, after all, admit to her participation in a plot to murder her daughter. Accepted Drager's protection and considered doing his bidding. And now that Everett is gone, she can't help but hold Domanso at least partly responsible.

She feels the heat in her chest all over again at the thought of it. As instructed, she drives to the local address Maureen provided by text, a health promotion building if she is not mistaken.

She supposes that makes sense, the woman was a DHP agent, no one will question her presence on site, and it will afford both of them some discretion. Under any other circumstance, she would even be excited for the opportunity to tour the division.

She parks in the guest agent lot, pulls at the rearview mirror until she can see her reflection, musses at her bangs, checks her teeth for lipstick and then takes a deep breath and exits the car. She makes her way to the main entrance at an energetic pace, thankful for her sensible shoes.

The wind is brisk today, biting into her cheeks, hinting at the change of season. She turns her face away, shuffling sideways to the foyer, feeling instant relief as she steps through the double glass doors into the lobby and a waiting Maureen Domanso.

"Sandra," is all she says by way of greeting.

"Maureen."

Sandra checks herself, forces the hostility from her tone.

"I assume given we could not chat over the phone that this is related to our earlier discussion. I assure you; I have not changed my mind. I will see this through. For my daughter," she adds as a bitter reminder.

"And for my son," Maureen states quietly.

Sandra's animosity dissolves. She realizes that the Domanso family is also a victim of Vladimir Draeger's machinations. Maureen shakes the melancholy, stiffens her back and resumes her business persona.

"There is a reason I needed to see you here, in person. Please, follow me."

A sense of foreboding charges the atmosphere as Sandra follows, matching the click of Domanso's four-inch heels echoing down the hallway. She halts abruptly in front of a nondescript door made of solid wood, impermeable. A health promotion agent lingers nearby. Maureen dispenses with the young man with a peremptory order.

"Cole, retrieve this morning's lab report for the patient."

"Right away, Ms. Domanso."

The coltish young man heads toward the stairwell without pause.

She just said, "The patient." Sandra flashes back to Everett's stay at a DHP site, not this one, but similar. Her heart sinks, she knows what she is about to see on the other side.

The heavy door falls behind them as they enter the bedchamber. Sandra feels like she's been locked in a tomb.

The boy lay motionless, draped in a blue infirmary gown, covered to the waist with a thin flannel sheet. Just like Everett, the repetitive beeping and hypnotic rise and fall of the atrial fibrillation monitor fills the room. Just like

Everett, the boy is deep in sleep. But where Everett's injuries were a mystery, this boy might have been mauled by a mountain lion.

"Oh my, you poor child," Sandra laments.

"Bees," Maureen states simply.

Sandra looks at her in confusion.

"We stopped counting at two thousand five hundred," she can tell Sandra is still confounded. "Stings that is."

"Oh, dear me," Sandra shakes her head. "Who is he?"

Maureen cocks her head, "I was hoping you could tell me."

"What? Why would I know this boy?"

He is truly unrecognizable with all the bruising and swelling.

"I'm working on a theory," Maureen replies. "His name is Pedro Ramón; he is an education and research agent from the southwest quadrant."

She picks up a tablet from the small desk lining the wall and offers it to Sandra.

"This is a more," she hesitates, searching for the right word. "Unobstructed likeness of the boy."

Sandra takes the tablet. The familiarity is indubitable, but it takes her a moment to reconcile the agent's smiling face with a context.

"I *do* recognize him. From the annual conference, the last two conferences more precisely. This is—" she looks up at Maureen and swallows, the woman's *theory* suddenly making the leap into Sandra's head.

"This is Everett's friend," she pronounces with a note of finality.

Maureen approaches the boy and brushes the hair from his damp forehead with uncharacteristic tenderness. Her final question echoes in Sandra's mind.

"All connected, as I suspected. So, what does Draeger want with you now, Pedro Ramón?"

Dr. Draeger glares at the documents in his hand until they combust, then watches the flames lick at the edges, the pages curling in on themselves. He lets the fire caress his fingertips until it has consumed its prey. The ash falls like rain onto the desktop.

This feeling of betrayal is so foreign to him, he cannot name it at first. Human emotion is so, enervating. And to think he felt some semblance of regret for terminating Mr. Ashton. He'd actually allowed himself to, like the man.

His assistant procured his DNA; a glass, a pen, a computer keyboard, who knows? He'd acquired a sample and tested it against Father's DNA. And sent the results to José Castillo.

Well, at least he'd snuffed out the old agent before he could disseminate his findings. But now the Ramón boy knows, and who else? No one will ever follow him if they learned who, what, he is. His authority will lose legitimacy, he will be exposed. The truth must never be revealed; he is Dr. Vladimir Draeger, most esteemed senior agent, in service to the Biodome.

Another thought gives him pause. Father will be most cross when he learns of this latest development. He must not jeopardize the plan. Father is counting on him to continue sowing the seeds of impiety here on Earth while he erases the Beginning, trapping man in a perpetual state of moral profligacy. Father will find a way around the existential virus; he is certain of it. For his part, failure is not an option.

Draeger hangs up the phone. Dr. Levine confirmed that the boy was found, alive, and brought to the Midwest division health promotion complex where he is receiving treatment for his injuries. So, against all odds, the boy breathes.

Another phone call to the DHP, the lead nursing agent, one Samantha O'Hara fumbling over her responses to his litany of questions.

"Yes, Sir. Pedro is physically stabilized but has yet to regain consciousness."

"Well, Sir, we lost count after two thousand five hundred."

"No, Sir, he is comatose, but his brain function is intact."

"Of course, Sir, we will alert you the moment the agent wakes."

Draeger ends the call with a sense of trepidity tinged with relief. He sleeps and is therefore silent, but his intuition is sounding alarm bells. He's been afforded some much-needed time to reaffirm his control and yet…

Stop.

A little self-reproach is in order, he decides.

Stop chasing shadows. The boy just surpassed a centuries-old world record, anybody in his position would be asleep.

Chapter 16

'In all fighting, the direct method may be used for joining battle, but indirect methods will be needed in order to secure victory.'

—Sun Tzu, The Art of War

I sit in between Jake and Pedro, our campfire casting dancing shadows all around us in the moonlight. The way the boys banter back and forth, they could be childhood BFFs. Leave it to Jake to make my friend feel welcome.

As they swap stories about mishaps and misfortunes from their early years, it strikes me that they are as similar as they are different. And somehow, they complete each other. Both attractive. No, way more than that. I flashback to the 99 P.C. spelling bee championships at my old high school. Thomas Bellwood claimed the victory. I can see him now, concentration furrowing his brow, sweat tickling his upper lip.

"Definition, please."

The pronouncer looked down her nose at the nervous teen and recited.

"Pulchritudinous: having extraordinary physical beauty."

I remember choking on a laugh, that was so not what I was expecting, it sounded more like a puss-filled sore. But the word stuck, and now I have occasion to use it. Both Jake and Pedro are *pulchritudinous*, but where Jake is an Adonis, especially now, Pedro is more subtle at first glance, more Vitruvian.

And likewise, both sagacious, but in this case, Pedro's hyperintelligence is like a beacon in a storm where it might be easy to underestimate Jake. And they share a kindness, authenticity and compassion that wrap around me like a security blanket.

Lulled by the heat of the fire and the sound of light conversation, I'm halfway to dreamland when Achilles howls somewhere in the darkness. He's been hunting for a while now. Usually, he will tiptoe back to camp and plop down at our side, licking his jaws to indicate he is sated. Jake is on his feet instantly, Pedro right behind him, the lackadaisical ambience gone in the snap of a finger.

"Evey," I hear the concern in Jake's voice, "that sounds like a warning."

Three sharp barks confirm his appraisal of the situation.

Jake works fast as lighting. He pulls a green bough from a nearby tree, ripping the three-inch limb from the trunk without a hint of difficulty and peels away the offshoot branches.

He removes bark from a downy birch tree, rolls it in the sap from a massive pine, and wraps it around the end of the stick. Rustling through the dirt, he comes up with handfuls of dry grass and dead leaves and stuffs it underneath the bark. Ninety seconds later, we have a flaming torch and Jake is leading us to Achilles and the anonymous threat our wolf has discovered.

We follow the snarling and barking into the night, Jake leading with the torch in one hand, his other in mine, and my other hand clasped firmly in Pedro's, an unbreakable human chain. I see Achilles first, the brilliant white of his fur stands out against the gloom.

His back is to us, and in a few more steps I can see the hackles on his shoulders, the flattened ears, the wide, predatory stance. Nothing moves. The torch envelops us in a halo, but as we move in closer, it sheds enough light that I can just make out a large grey prominence directly in front of him. The wolf's predacious instincts have been triggered by a rock?

I release the compression on my back teeth, I didn't even realize I was clenching, and loosen my grip on both hands.

"Really boy?" I tease Achilles, "You dragged us out here and took five years off my life for this?"

But the wolf does not relent. Both Jake and Pedro redouble their hold on my hands at the same time. Jake pulls us closer, lifting the torch high in the air. We all look up together, moving as one.

Fear does all kind of crazy up and down my spine as I look into the face of a Megalosaurus-sized man, made entirely of stone.

"It is a statue?" Pedro inquires in his affirmative.

"But where did it come from? Who built it? When?" Jake is flustered.

"Boys, it's the middle of the night," I reason.

"Why don't we come back tomorrow morning, you know, when we can actually see the thing?"

Jake and Pedro acknowledge my logic with a couple of light shrugs.

"Achilles? Please?"

The wolf turns at the sound of his name and trots over to me. I ruffle his thick neck.

"Okay, it's decided. First, we sleep, then we sleuth."

Dawn stretches across the eastern horizon. I groan, roll over onto my back and crack an eye. Jake is already pacing, Achilles mimicking his movements. He is always considerate, he didn't want to wake me, even though he is itching to get going.

I spot Pedro sitting by our now defunct fire, a large rock in one hand, a smaller one in the other. He's absorbed in the repetitive tapping of one against the other. Great, two early risers. And then there's me.

I clamber to my feet, arrange my boxy shift, finger comb my hair and throw it into a braid, tied off with one of the little vines I've been collecting in my pocket. Jake stops pacing.

"What do you say we head back and check out rock man? We can pick up breakfast along the way?"

Pedro tucks the two rocks into the hollow of our tree trunk bench.

"The ancient Inuit called it an *inunnguaq,* built to guide travelers. Or to warn them. It is a mystery how one came to be here."

Without being asked, Achilles leads the way back through the thicket. We enter the little clearing. Trampled saplings and two large depressions in the soft soil are evidence enough that a massive, heavy entity sat on this very spot. But the statue, rock man, *inunnguaq*…whatever you want to call it, is gone.

We look at each other in stunned silence, none of us wanting to put to words what we must all be thinking. A soft breeze wafts through the clearing and Achilles is on high alert. He's picked up a scent. Five seconds later, he takes off at a lope. I look at Jake and Pedro.

"Do we follow?" I ask with my eyes.

They both look dubious. Finally, Jake calls out to the wolf.

"Hey, wait up!"

He doesn't go far. Crouching deep, the wolf goes very still, except for the involuntary twitch of ears. I hear it now too; a raspy, hissing sound, low to the ground. Like a flash, Achilles pounces.

I recoil as a wake of vultures erupts from the trees with a high-pitched scream that lifts the hair off the back of my neck. Thirty, maybe more, organize into formation as they climb into the air and flee from Achilles, our king of predators.

New sounds reach my ears, sounds that make my skin crawl. Ripping, crunching, the distinct snapping of bones. With Jake and Pedro beside me, we brush aside the heavy growth and I think I might be sick.

A family of whitetail deer, a big buck, the more delicate doe and three fawns, all butchered. Two decapitated, another's limbs torn off, and the smallest one completely eviscerated. The buck's rack is torn from its skull and broken into pieces like tinder. Deliberately cruel. The only natural thing about the gruesome scene is our wolf, taking over where the vultures left off.

Jake is quiet, almost withdrawn. Unlike the fox, the deer were not diseased, did not succumb to the pestilence and bacteria proliferating in this incessant heat. We couldn't very well punish Achilles for feasting on the remains, besides I'm not sure how well that would have gone over. Sorry boy, we're going to bury your seven-course meal here, hope you don't mind.

Jake took the skins, explaining that once the hair fell off, we would fashion the leather into clothing and shoes. Then he collected the antlers, even the smallest shards.

These we will use for utensils and tools. A hair comb would be nice. Without explanation, Pedro asked if he could keep one of the two large shafts. I've no doubt he has a purpose in mind, but I don't press. We're all a little dejected.

We sit around the cold fire pit, immersed in our own thoughts. I barely taste breakfast. Without the sweet berries, the nuts, roots and leaves all blend together. I'm not complaining, my hair and skin glow and my muscles are thriving from the dense nutrition and protein in our natural diet. The fructose is just a bonus.

I notice that new fruit is sprouting around our camp. Though still unripe, it is free of bugs and those gross little white worms thanks to the bees that have set up a perimeter around us. Another parting gift from the Empress.

The shock of the slaughter overshadows our disappearing giant problem. Since it doesn't appear either boy wants to address the proverbial elephant in the room, I clear my throat and break the silence.

"Ugh, any thoughts on, you know, the missing rock formation?"

Pedro is bent over his knees, back at it with those rocks. He's moved on to honing the edges of the larger stone, dragging it repetitively over the smaller one. A tool of some sort, for cutting, I think. It will definitely come in handy.

My question stays his hands but he keeps his head bowed. Jake is on hands and knees, scraping remnants of flesh from the deer skins with a piece of shale. The set of his shoulders, the rancor in his mannerisms as he attacks the pelts, the blood he draws on his fingers, all speak to his mood. The contempt rolls off of him.

I kneel down beside him and put my hands over his. They are shaking.

"Jake," I say softly. "You have to let it go."

He heaves a huge sigh and slumps.

"I know, I'm working on it," he concedes.

"Guys," I include Pedro now. "We need to figure this out."

Jake engages first.

"The volcano, the water, the heat, the pestilence, the animals—" he pauses, "I can't explain that rock monster, but the tetra, this *Abaddon* you call him, he is not trying to kill me anymore, he's trying to kill the garden. And succeeding."

"*Si*," Pedro agrees. "*Guerra indireta.*"

Jake and I both stare. Jake is about to interject when I put a hand on his chest.

"Wait for it," I advise, speaking quietly out of the side of my mouth.

As if on cue, Pedro continues.

"Indirect warfare. He is using a strategy employed by the ancients in their endless military conquests. Weaken your enemy by upsetting his equilibrium. Only then do you engage in the direct offensive. *Si,* it is a most excellent approach."

"Well, I'm glad you approve," I squint at my own sarcasm. "So much for hometown advantage."

Jake responds with a dangerous edge in his voice, "Well I'm done with this reptile wrecking ball. And I'm done running. We need a little offensive strategy of our own."

I don't disagree.

"As far as I can see, there's only one way. We don't have the luxury of a tacit assault. We need a direct hit."

They have found His golem thanks to that oversized dog. No matter, He still has the element of surprise, they are none the wiser to its origin. More importantly, they've no idea that it is his Frankenstein. Nonetheless, they *have* divined his surreptitious infiltration.

The Chosen One might have figured it out but the Third legitimized his observation with his intuitive analysis of ancient military strategy. This is a serious development. It has prompted them to contemplate a counteroffensive.

Once they settled back into their camp, He had watched and waited. When they finally gave in to exhaustion, the wolf included, He worked with stealth, relocating the golem deep in the recess of a crag on the east side of a narrow mountain pass a few short miles to the north of their camp.

Considerably well camouflaged, He was satisfied that it would not be so easily discovered. He's spent the remainder of the night devising a plan to keep them on the defensive. He will compel the trio to move into the pass. He on one side, His golem on the other. A rockslide, or two, in between. Assured victory.

They are scattered, but they are many. He calls to them, den by den, pit by pit. First His *Scolecophidia* clade; hundreds of nests of fossorial thread snakes, and many more primitive blind snakes, like overgrown earthworms, slither out from their underground burrows.

His more evolved *Alethinophidia*; pipe snakes, split jaws, mud snakes, keep-backs, and more, all eager to answer the Master's call.

Finally, his most advanced, deadly *Caenophidians*. His pit vipers, His mambas, thousands of members of his *colubrid* family, dipsadines, natricines, rats, twigs, milk, reed snakes, and even his vicious boomslangs, all assemble under his banner.

He organizes his army for the offensive, flanking the east and west, assembling his front line on the south side. Hemming them in, forcing them to move north, forcing them into the pass.

I wake to the slowing drip of water from the overhang Jake has built to protect us. The three, no, make that four of us, are crammed in between the roots of our new tree, waiting out the rain.

A blessing and a curse at the same time, these downpours. A necessary evil, if we are to survive this heat. I must have dozed off, comforted as I am by Jake and Pedro and Achilles surrounding me and in the safety of our shelter.

"Is it stopping?" I ask.

We must have been cooped up in here for a few hours now.

"Yes, sleeping beauty, it's petering out," Jake mocks me.

Pedro chuckles, "*Si, bela Adormecida.*"

He's rubbing Achilles in long strokes down his spine. The wolf is basking in the attention, head held high, eyes half closed, tongue lolling from the side of his mouth.

"I wasn't sleeping," I fib. "I was just resting my eyes."

Jake and Pedro look at each other and burst out laughing.

"Uh huh," Jake counters playfully. "And the open-mouthed snoring? Just resting your jaw and tongue?"

I am mortified. "I do not *snore*," I emphasize the word like it's an ailment.

More snickers from the peanut gallery. Even Achilles looks at me mockingly.

"Hardy har har. If you two, or three," Achilles is happy to be included, "are quite done making fun of me, I am going to scout for our dinner."

I don't wait for more teasing. I poke my head out from under the canopy, confirm that the sky is letting up, and climb out. The boys are right behind me. I resist the urge to stretch, no sense giving them more *let's make fun of Evey*, ammo.

I screw up my eyes as I look up ahead. Am I seeing things? The heat must be getting to me. Like a fluttering mirage, the land looks to be moving in ripples through the light fog that always comes with the rain. But when the boys go very still beside me and Achilles lets out a warning snarl, I know they see what I see.

We stand transfixed as the earth tremor rolls toward us, still obscured by the thick mist. The illusion of solid ground abandoning me under my feet is giving me vertigo. Closer, closer, it breaks through the haze. I don't even realize I'm screaming.

Chapter 17

'Things are not always what they seem; the first appearance deceives many; the intelligence of a few perceives what has been carefully hidden.'
—Phaedrus c. 444–393 BC

Hundreds, no, thousands of them. Tiny ones at the front, no more than a few inches, with see-through skin mixed in with others the color of ink. They move in from three sides, like a giant *V*, fifty feet deep. Behind the odd little beasts, more recognizable ones with the telltale scales of their species.

A parade of different lengths and colorings but relatively similar in stature. And then, overshadowing the entire procession from the rear, the giants; the distinct diamond-shaped heads and slitted pupils of the deadliest of their kind.

"Everett, Everett!" A light slap on my cheek. Jake comes into focus. "We have to go. Now!"

My eyes are automatically drawn back to the army of snakes inching toward us. I stand here, immobilized by equal parts fear and revulsion, while Jake and Pedro rummage through the camp, picking up anything we can carry. Jake grabs the two smaller leather pelts and stuffs them in my hand.

He grabs small items and shoves them in the pockets of my shift then fills his own hands. Pedro has picked up the large antler he's been fiddling with incessantly, it's poking out from under his shirt, hooked onto his pants. Everything moves in slow motion. I'm numb, I imagine this is what it feels like to drown.

Jake tugs me by the arm, forcing me to move. My legs feel like cement as we scuttle over the uneven terrain. I trip once, twice, it snaps me out of this stupor, and I consciously suppress my fear response. We're being herded north, the only opening we have. Achilles is not even protesting; he knows as well as we do that to stand is to die.

"He's changed tactics," Pedro notes between short breaths, still computing despite the adrenaline overload.

Jake hasn't even broken a sweat. He shoots Pedro a look over his shoulder. "What?"

"Something has changed. He has become impatient perhaps. Or angry?"

"Or both," I grumble.

"Does it matter?" Jake is positively cantankerous. "We have to keep moving!"

We are outpacing the advancing menace. But to what end? We can't run forever.

"There!" through the thinning forest, Jake points to a mountain range up ahead.

"If we can get up the side of one of those rocky mountains, we can find a narrow ledge. Even if they follow, we have a halfway decent defensive position. We can keep them at bay until we figure out our next move."

It sounds desperate, but I'm not seeing any other options. And I for one, cannot continue at this pace much longer. I glance sidelong at Pedro; his face is etched with skepticism but he nods to Jake to lead the way.

Right on schedule, He muses. They are winded but intact. He will let his minions loose once they reach the pass, not before. He expects nothing less than total discipline, particularly from his lethal rear guard, and they have not disappointed.

"Soon," He transmits, "you will hold formation until I release you."

The crush of serpents strains against the bonds imposed by the Master, but none break ranks. He instructs the flanks to close in, force the enemy into his death trap. *Like catching flies in a spiderweb.*

They slow to a jog, the female showing signs of fatigue, lingering aspects of distress and antipathy in her otherwise feeble affect, her skin waxy and complexion ashen. The Chosen One is almost dragging her behind him. The Third is managing remarkably well, his physical stamina belying his intellectual tendency.

She is rendered inconsequential; however, He must not underestimate either male. Or the dog. He lies in wait with growing satisfaction as they reach the base of the range and begin their ascent, perfectly positioned to enter the pass.

Pedro keeps pace with Jake, his mind churning in time with his gut. Something is telling him they are walking into an ambuscade. His thoughts automatically return to the Biodome, his time inside the Android. There is a clue there, just out of reach, niggling at the edge of his intuition.

This serpent army, such unnatural behavior for the species. The heat and humidity are causing so much decay in the soil, the vegetation putrefying from the infestation of insects of all types, the garden is practically composting itself. And because of this, the smell of ammonia hangs in the air.

Pedro's nostrils fill with the reek of it, a rancid combination of sweat and urine. He is acutely aware that this pnictogen hydride is the ultimate repellent for snakes, and yet, here they are. As though they are being compelled. As though their will were no longer their own. Just like, just like…

It plays out in his mind's eye; how could he not see it? It is a duplicate play. Except then it was a computer-generated legion of clones and this time it is a flesh and blood army. They stopped him last time by wiping out his programming.

He knows what he has to do.

Pedro is interrupted by Jake's terse command.

"First, we go in. And then, we go up."

They enter the narrow pass between the two tallest peaks of the range, scattering the jagged talus as they climb. The incline is steep, all three use their hands to assist in scaling the slope, a physically grueling climb. Even the wolf pants with the exertion.

Pedro wonders if it might not be more sensible to descend the pass and take their chances on the other side. One rearward glance cancels out the notion. The horde of bloodthirsty demons are not deterred by the challenging landscape, worming their way over, around, and in between the unstable footing, not closing the distance, but not increasing it either. No, Jake is right, they must go up.

"Take a quick breather," Jake instructs, peering up the leeward side of the pass. "We'll go up this side. I can see plenty of ledge rock up there."

Pedro understands. Jake is truly exceptional at reading this land. Everett is not so sure.

"But Jake, it's much smoother on the other side, wouldn't that make the climb easier?"

Jake shakes his head as he explains.

"That," he points, "is the windward slope. The wind has washed away all the loose scree. We will be battered the whole way up Evey, it will make the climb that much more treacherous."

Pedro nods approvingly. Jake looks like one of those macho soccer types he never much cared for growing up. What was it that his *avó* used to say about Dr. Castillo? *Never judge a book by its cover.* The aphorism applies to Jake as much as it did to his mentor. Smart grandmother.

Jake brings him back to the present with words of encouragement.

"It's not as bad as it looks. We've got this."

The trio are about to start their ascent when the advance from the south halts abruptly, the rustle and hiss of a chiliad of angry snakes drifting into silence on the soft wind. Everyone freezes mid-step. Achilles tilts his head at the sound of nothing.

In his peripheral vision, Pedro spies movement from a crevice in between two massive boulders on the descending side of the pass. At the same time, another flash of motility has him whipping his head back to the stationary army.

He has the most outlandish sense of self-satisfaction as the Destroyer emerges in the vanguard, his obedient troops awaiting the next order, while the giant *inunnguaq* lumbers into position at twelve o'clock.

I was right, it 'is' an ambush.

Chipping away at the faintest trace of uncertainty in the lead agent, Maureen pleads her case.

"Sir, the ancients used discursive and deliberative oratory extremely effectively. The inaugural speech and state of the union address were staples in the earliest political arsenal. The citizenry lapped it up every time. They need to hear you reassure them of your undying devotion and commitment to the welfare of the Biodome." She pauses before adding, "they grow restless."

Draeger considers.

"Restless? Have they forgotten what will befall them should they step out of line?"

So, he's still playing that card. Well, I suppose he can't acquiesce now, I would do the same.

Maureen shows no outward sign of agnosticism as she deliberates.

"Of course not, Sir. Everyone knows you control the existential virus on behalf of the Biodome. I am simply suggesting it as a means of pacifying the masses. A rallying call. As the ancients used to say, you can catch more flies with honey than with vinegar."

She waits, forcing herself to breathe.

"Hmmm," the hint of a smile appears on Draeger's lips.

"Yes, indeed, there have been some rather rousing, evocative public orations throughout human history. The Gettysburg Address, the Tilbury Speech, Their Finest Hour, I have a dream—" he is lost in time.

He stands and paces with the most expressive look on his face that Maureen has ever seen on the perpetually solemn man.

"Yes, Ms. Domanso, a splendid idea."

Maureen takes the compliment with diffidence.

"Thank you, Sir. I will get started on the speech right away. You will have a draft of key talking points by day's end."

Draeger clucks his tongue, the tiniest crease appearing between his eyebrows.

"That will not be necessary, Ms. Domanso. This will be a personal undertaking."

"Oh," Maureen is a bit stunned, Draeger never does anything himself.

"Very well. Sir. I will attend to the venue and schedule. Agents from across the Biodome are especially attentive on the weekend summary broadcasts, the next one being Friday. Is that too soon, Sir?"

"Two days is all the time I require. Why, the address is practically writing itself as we speak."

He is uncharacteristically ardent. Maureen capitalizes on the moment.

"I've no doubt, Sir. It will be arranged forthwith."

She makes to exit the office. Reaching for the door handle, she hesitates when he speaks at her back.

"Rest assured, I will most certainly outdo the forefathers."

She nods once and slips out without looking back. He cannot see the uncontained smile on her face as she commends herself. She exploited his pride and arrogance flawlessly.

He has no idea, he just walked into an ambush.

Draeger rolls the 24-karat-trimmed fountain pen back and forth between his fingers. He has been looking for a way to reaffirm his sovereignty since losing control of the existential virus.

That pesky human emotion, self-doubt, has been lingering around since he is returned. Of course, no one is the wiser, but it was much more elementary when he could punish at will. This subterfuge is tedious.

Domanso is astute. She took the temperature of the communal mindset, tepid, and conceived a sensible plan to improve public trust in his administration. She is right, it is a strategy with a very long tradition of success. And Father will accept nothing less than continued success.

Anything that will secure his, and by extension, Father's reign in the Age of Ascent, must be effectuated. Essentially, all it takes is eloquence and a silver tongue, and he has an abundance of the former and exudes the latter. He'll have them eating out of his hand.

I am gorgonized, both body and brain refusing to cooperate. The rock man, the statue, just stepped out in front of us, blocking any path forward. Its movements are stroppy and arduous, but the beast's bulk more than compensates for its sluggishness.

Behind us, the tetra stands front and center of the mass of snakes. They are suddenly subdued, every single one of them gone stock-still. It's as if time, and life itself, has paused altogether. No seconds, no minutes, no sensation, no breath. I'm numb.

I register something in my hands. I don't remember how it got there. My eyes are the only part of my body that move as I look down. My fingers are wrapped around an off-white shaft, about a foot long.

The fingers on my left-hand probe gritty little pits at the base of the shaft while my right-hand caresses silky veneer as the diameter of the shaft tapers off.

I watch my own hand gently glide up the shaft to the flint axe head embedded into the end of it, fastened with a sinewy material that I know to be organic. Animal tendon. And then it dawns on me, the shaft, a handle, also organic, an antler.

I turn it over, the light hitting the razor-sharp edge of the weapon, so perfectly honed it might as well have been machine-finished. A noise in the distance, growing louder. A voice, I can't quite make out the words. A violent shake.

"Everett, Miss Everett, *senhora*, please."

Pedro is squeezing my shoulders, tugging me back and forth. The world comes back into focus like a shockwave, overloading my senses all at once.

"*Senhora*, you must listen to me."

I blink. I see him. I hear him. He stoops down and brings his face close, his eyes searching mine. He knows I'm back. He lifts my hands, brings the axe, his axe, to eye level between us.

"Remember the Lernaean Hydra Everett?"

The Biodome, the Android. It feels like a thousand years ago. I nod, remembering the battle. My torso twitches involuntarily, I can feel the life being squeezed out of me all over again, like a phantom pain. Pedro shakes me, snapping me out of it. Again.

"I remember," is all I can muster.

"This time, you will be Hercules," he taps the axe.

"What? What do you mean Pedro? How? When?" I am reduced to a bumbling idiot.

His gentle, serene smile calms my racing heart.

"You will know."

Pedro takes the axe from my hands and proceeds to fashion a belt from the deer skin I've just tossed to the side, thinking it would do us no good now. The blade cuts through the hide like butter. I don't move while he ties the strip of leather around my waist and then holsters the axe on my left hip.

Jake calls out, "time to go."

All hell breaks loose.

Chapter 18

'The past lies like a nightmare upon the present.'

—Karl Marx

The look of utter shock and dismay on their faces is worth the price of admission. He takes a brief moment to savor their terror, it tinges the air like a redolent Romanée-Conti Pinot Noir, filling him with thoughts of home. Soon. His work here is almost finished. So predictable, it was almost too easy.

The Chosen One thinks to scale the side of the mountain, examining the face, looking for handholds and footholds. He hopes to find refuge in the precipices. He is trying to convince the wolf to run, to save himself, but the Waheela will have none of it. He sits firmly at the boy's side, loyal to the end.

Meanwhile, a heartwarming scene; the Third is handing off his only weapon to the female in a pathetic display of altruism. She is the weak link, He knows it, and apparently so do they. How quaint, a little pep talk. He cannot make out the words, but the girl affirms the message of encouragement with those chaste eyes of hers.

The boy cuts a strip from one of the pelts they have now discarded and secures the halberd around her waist, the head of the weapon resting just above her hip bone, trapped over the firm knot the boy has made in the leather. Little good that will do her.

When the trio, and the wolf, taking a slightly different path, have ascended the first ten feet, he binds himself to the golem. The beast trudges to the base of the mountain, its head at par with their feet. It slams down hard with a foot. Again.

It packs a punch into the side of the mountain. The female loses her grip first, her foot slips and she dangles, precariously close to falling. The Chosen One reaches down, grasps her by the forearm and in one smooth motion, hauls her up. She reattaches herself to the rockface. Disappointing.

He sets the golem to work anew, with more force this time. The mountain shakes with the battering, loose rock from above begins to rain down. This time the Third lets go first just before a great slab of rock sheers him in two.

He tumbles back into the pass, rolling to a stop on hands and knees. The girl is next, no rescue this time. She reverses course, slowing her descent. And finally, the Chosen One leaps, landing with a grace and agility that only he could achieve. He crouches like a cougar ready to strike.

His little avalanche creates an embankment of serrated rubble, making another attempt at climbing that much more difficult. He notes with delight that the wolf is nowhere to be seen. Perhaps He has taken care of one problem already.

There is a physical cost, of course, as the somnolence begins a slow creep into his cells, reminding him to pace himself. He stations the golem for the moment, turning his attention to his tarried army.

You have been most patient, however, I do have but one more task before I restore your freedom. Destroy them.

Released from their catatonic prison, the serpents advance as one roiling, irascible mob. The most dangerous among them quickly overrun their kin in their lust for blood. The three make for the other side of the pass in a desperate attempt at evasion.

Tut tut.

No longer concerned with his own vitality, He throws everything at them at once. He shores up the energy required to invigorate the golem, sending it racing back to block the pass, swooping down with enormous stone mitts to swipe at the threesome. They barely dodge the strike.

The snakes are upon them, clambering one over the other, daring one another to strike. *Yes, my children, feast.* He shrouds them in appetence like an aphrodisiac, draws more hellfire with reckless abandon, as much as required to fuel the onslaught. He will not lose.

Maureen checks her stage set. A crisp midnight blue backdrop with the Biodome flag emblazoned across the top and three words written in bold script underneath: Honesty, Integrity, Purpose. The cameras trained on the lectern, an image of the humanoid at the center of the Biodome tastefully carved into the wood.

A trick ancient politicians borrowed from the clergy. Raise yourself above the masses and somehow you are an authority, a virtuoso, more than those at your feet. At least the clerics were ordained by God and held to a higher standard of moral obedience. Ideologically anyway.

Two long tables draped in the same midnight blue fabric offset with pale grey chairs line both sides of the center stage, one for each cabinet member. To give the people, and more importantly, Dr. Draeger, the illusion of solidarity.

Stage lights with just the right amount of filtering to wash the room in a warm ambience with spotlights making the guest of honor the undisputed focal point. She is just completing the final sound check when Draeger walks in. A queasiness washes over her as she grasps the gravity of what she has orchestrated.

Draeger peruses the chamber, running a slender finger along one of the long tables leading to the lectern, a look of satisfaction about him. A young agent pushes a stainless-steel cart into the room, setting a small glass in front of each chair and two large water decanters on each table. Two more agents set up row upon row of chairs in the gallery.

Using the agent database from the last annual conference, Maureen sent out personal invitations to dozens of senior agents from various departments. It would be construed as impolite to decline the solicitation, and no one wants to offend Dr. Draeger. Maureen is confident the seats will be filled. She is counting on it.

"Sir. Is the room to your liking?"

She checks her watch before adding, "there is time yet, of course, I can make any last-minute changes as you see fit."

She hears her own kowtowing. Best to remain incisive but deferential.

"This will do, Ms. Domanso." Draeger seems, preoccupied.

At exactly fifteen minutes to the hour, the cabinet members enter the chamber single file, taking their respective places at the tables. Maureen scowls at the trepidation cloying the air, silently entreating the agents to get their emotions under control. If she can smell the fear on them, then so can Draeger.

Only a few raise their eyes to hers, Henry, Gary, prudish Edith. The rest of them toy with pens, run fingers along the rims of their water glasses, position and reposition themselves in their seats. You could cut the nervous tension with a knife.

The swinging of the back door as guest agents pour into the room has the opposite effect, their excited chatter and liveliness diffusing the doom and gloom. Maureen takes a head count, pleased with the turnout. There are at least 25 agents filling up the chairs. All except one partake in the handshakes and small talk. Sandra Steele takes her seat in the front row.

I don't know where to look next. We have nowhere to go. The stone abomination is hurling boulders the size of small cars at us from behind, slow enough that we can avoid being decimated, but fast enough that we have to keep watching over our shoulders.

"Pedro, your left!" Jake yells as another one comes sailing in our direction.

He shifts just in time.

We face forward, snakes coming at us from all directions. I feel the bite on my ankle before I can step out of the way. My heart sinks. This is it then. Pedro and Jake are beside me in a flash. Pedro is animated.

"*Senhora*, it is a ball python, it is not venomous."

I have never been so happy to hear I've been bitten by a python. Pedro addresses Jake and I together now.

"Watch for triangular heads, thick bodies, those are the dangerous ones."

Easier said than done. I don't know about Pedro, but that python looked pretty thick to me. They are attacking each other as much as us. Such a universal trait, turning on one's own kind for advantage. I almost laugh at the idea. Man is no more evolved than a snake.

But like man, the larger, more powerful diamond heads are crushing their weaker counterparts. Although there are less of these deadly carnivores, our demise is imminent now.

I've just about given up when I hear a vicious growl as Achilles pounces in front of us from a high point in the settling mountain side. His beautiful coat is blood-stained on his left flank where he is injured but he does not relent, swaying left and right, snarling, feigning attacks with quick jerky movements that cause the snakes to pause. He is the only thing standing between us and certain death.

Two identical hooded king cobras, characteristically flattened along the head and neck, morph into fifteen feet of bloated body and pointed tails. They slither in tandem toward Achilles. Black, ringed with silver their full length, they move in perfect synchrony, it's like watching a choreographed dance routine.

I am mesmerized. That is, until they rear up, exposing vicious fangs and a sickly green underside. I don't remember drawing the axe, but it is in my hands. Without thinking, I step in front of the wolf and swing with everything I've got.

I connect right at the heart of each of them, the first two feet of snake goes whipping through the air while arterial spray mists my face and hair as the organs beat once, twice, before coming to rest, the blood now draining in a shallow pool between the rocks.

This is the first time I've ever taken life away from anything, ever. I had to choose, and I chose Achilles. I don't have time to feel, or to consider my actions any further than this.

The giant is closing in behind us, lifting those tree trunk legs high in the air, ancient military style. It means to stomp us out like wayward embers. Again, all I see is defeat.

Jake and Achilles have its attention, they draw it away from me, running a zig-zag pattern in front of it that seems to confuse the monster. It teeters, tripping over its own feet as it pounds the earth with a force that I feel in the back of my teeth. I am left standing with this bloody hatchet as more wicked snakes invade the pass.

I dance, I swing, I jump, I swing, over and over, but any hope I may have harbored is draining away along with the little remaining strength I have left in this body. Out of the corner of my eye, I spot it. No, Him. Coiled atop a large boulder with a bird's eye view of the chaos. Not a care in the world. He almost looks like he's sleeping.

Pedro scrutinizes the tetra, spiraled around itself, unmoving. Perched high above the fray, the führer commanding his troops. And like every infamous ancient dictator, this puppet master has no intention of getting his hands dirty. He grits his teeth and bears down on his resolve. Time to cut the strings.

At exactly 2 p.m., Maureen steps to the lectern, calling the assembly to order. She tries, and fails, to ignore Sandra's stare, tries, and fails, to stop her involuntary swallow reflex. She reaches for a glass of water and sips in an attempt to disguise her discomfort. Draeger is none the wiser, self-absorbed and regaling in the attention.

She cues the mic with a light tap, makes eye contact with the two media agents manning the cameras, and then, begins her address.

"Welcome." The shuffling and prattling ceases. "This is a momentous event in the New Order. As my esteemed colleagues and I continue to serve the needs of every man, woman, and child in the Biodome," she pauses while the cameras pan over the tables flanking her. The cabinet members sit up straighter, chins tilting upward.

"Our commander-in-chief sets the bar for all with his unwavering devotion to our one nation. With magnanimity and asceticism, intellection and assertiveness, he inspires us to rise to new heights, both as individuals and as communities within the great Biodome."

She's laying it on thick, glimpsing Draeger where he sits in the shadows, waiting to be called to the stage. He is preening. She stops herself just before rolling her eyes. Her sycophancy is so convincing that Henry and Gary exchange glances under furrowed brows, uncertainty abducting them.

Hold the line, she begs in silence.

She glances stage left toward Draeger, chin in the air, arrogance rolling off him like a pompous peacock. *Just a little longer*, she reminds herself. She is so going to enjoy bursting his bubble.

"I have the great pleasure of introducing the keeper of our great nation, our protector, our savior. Please join me in welcoming Dr. Vladimir Draeger to share his words of wisdom and his vision for the future of the Biodome."

The agents break out in applause. Maureen eyes Sandra, thankful the woman is clapping to blend in, but notices her movements are slow and wooden.

The room sobers as an imperious Draeger breezes onto the stage. He approaches the lectern, his expression enigmatic. He offers no civilities nor gratitude for the introduction.

He pauses a moment and looks directly into the camera, his features going hard, callous. Maureen imagines that every single person watching is intimidated. His commanding baritone only adds to the effect.

"Before we look to the future, let us reflect on how far we've come."

He pauses, subtle dramatic flair. Silence hangs in the air.

"The ancients. So naïve. Such flawed thinking. They never could see the most obvious truth about humanity. It is not what man *does* that matters, it is who man *is*. The man-made rule of law was destined to fail. And fail it did, time and time again. And what did the ancients do?" he twirls a hand in the air, a gesture of levity.

"Why, make more rules, of course. Impose more restrictions, enact more laws," he lets the sentiment linger in the thick air.

"Such fools. They controlled not a whit. All the laws in the world were never going to stop the downfall. In fact, it only hastened the demise. Do you not see how perfectly sin evolved as civilization evolved?"

"As society became more and more oppressive, man became more disenfranchised, more cynical, more enraged. It was a self-fulfilling prophecy, the perfect ouroboros. A never-ending cycle of self-destruction and failed attempts at re-creation."

The silence turns sullen.

"Not once did the ancients stop and reflect on their endless miscarriages. Blinded by their own egocentricity. The very things that the rulers contrived; class wars, race wars, identity politics, gender politics, on and on and on, all dry tinder for the tiniest kernel of sin embedded in every human heart."

"Not only did they start the fire, they fanned the flames shamelessly throughout the centuries. A better soul despoiler there could never be."

The room goes stock-still and a chill runs down the back of Maureen's silk blouse. *That acerbic start is way more vinegar than honey.* Maureen imagines that families sitting around their televisions all around the world have a similar slack-jawed reaction to Draeger's opening. He seems oblivious to the impact of his words as he carries on.

"With the Correction and subsequent birth of the Biodome, all the wrongs perpetrated by man against his fellow man were eradicated, the boorish police state replaced with an omnipotence that is immune from the moral decay that seems to plague men wherever they go. Problem solved."

He places both hands on the lectern and leans into the microphone.

"And yet…over one hundred years later, the Biodome's disciplinarian is still meting out justice, the existential virus is active as ever. Such a disappointment."

He stands tall now.

"And so, after careful deliberation, the Biodome relented, acceding its authority. To me. It will forever remain our sovereign, but in name only. I sully my hands, for you, I carry the burden, for you. I dispense with the reprobates, for you."

"I stand before you today and pledge myself to you. I am your humble servant. I will see to it that we all live in harmony and with integrity and purpose. By whatever means necessary."

He heaves a big sigh and bows his head in supplication.

Who's the one laying it on thick now?

This time Maureen can't stop the eye roll. But as she looks at the smiling, fawning faces in the audience, she can see they've fallen for his fecundity. Hook, line, and sinker.

If the response from these senior agents is any indication, the only thing she's accomplished today in in defying Draeger. She swallows the hard lump in her throat, her little contrivance on the verge of backfiring. Badly. She forces a weak smile as the camera zooms out for a panoramic shot.

A self-effacing Draeger steps away from the lectern, even a few cabinet members appear captivated by his performance. The room breaks out in gregarious applause that continues for several long seconds, morphing into a standing ovation.

After several nods of approval, agents strike up conversations amongst themselves, the room falling into disarray as agents move in and out of small groups. A few cabinet members join in on the exchanges, today's purpose completely forgotten. Maureen watches in horror as her allies desert her.

The din of a dozen voices all talking at the same time is abruptly arrested when a strange sound comes over the loudspeaker. Everyone stops and stares at the lectern. The cameras swivel to the stage in an instant.

Sandra Steele stands at the lectern, her hands coming together in a golf clap dripping with condescension. Clap…clap…clap…clap, over and over, her face a vacant mask, giving nothing away. The repetitive sound echoes through the speakers. When the room is quiet, she opens with a single word.

"Nonsense."

Maureen looks for Draeger, he is on his feet, a look of utter astonishment on his face. She walks over and places herself between him and the lectern. He will have to shove her out of the way if he wants to get to Sandra and with the cameras broadcasting live, it is a risk he will not take. She hopes.

They lock eyes, she uses hers to point at the cameras, a look of pleading on her face, letting him think she is protecting him. He scowls, yielding to her warning.

Everyone stands completely motionless and owl-eyed as if the shock has robbed them of all motor skills and mental faculties. Sandra is undeterred.

"Puhlease—" she draws out the word, infusing it with sarcasm. "Are you really buying what Dr. Draeger is selling?"

She copies Draeger's move and glares into the camera, challenging every citizen in the Biodome as much as the agents standing an arm's length away.

"Since the Correction, we've but one, and only one, true leader. Non-human, but sentient nonetheless, the Biodome loves and cares for every one of us. I cannot explain its manifestation any more or any less than any of us. But I do know this. Because it is once removed from the temptations that plague the heart of man, it keeps the human condition in check. Do you honestly believe it would just give up on us, as Dr. Draeger claims? There is one small truth, I will grant him that much." She waits just a beat.

"Humans cannot lead humans while there is a crack in the moral armor. It will always, without fail, be exploited by those with the power and skill to manipulate, to lie, to cheat, to steal, for their own private ends."

She gives Draeger a look of disgust.

"And yet, we do exactly that, and willingly no less? Cannot you not see what will happen if we keep down this path, with this, imposter, this charlatan, as our leader? Are we so arrogant, so simple-minded, to expect anything will be different this time?"

"The existential virus is here because we brought it upon ourselves! We need it as plainly as we need air to breathe. But we must never, ever, allow her to be wielded by any man. She will become a twisted tool manipulated for nothing more than power and control."

She takes a deep breath, grabs hold of the wooden stand, her knuckles going white under the strain.

"We have failed time and again, to lead, and to be led, in the name of justice and goodwill, the historical record is sufficiently probative in this regard. We are not ready. I don't know that we will ever be ready. I won't be part of it. I reject Dr. Draeger as our leader." Another pause and then she closes.

"I am taking a stand right here, right now. He will bring us all down, he will bring back all the wrongs of the past, he will undo all that the Biodome has done for us. I would rather he strike me down than to continue to live in fear, to become a casualty of this tyranny. To live as the ancients lived."

Oh, dear Lord, Maureen tells herself. She pulls herself together, she has a part to play here.

She feigns abhorrence, turning to Draeger, stammering on her words.

"The, insolence! How dare she speak of you this way! We will all enjoy watching her suffer for her impudence, Sir."

She waits, holding her breath. If she is wrong, she may as well have twisted the knife in Sandra Steele's back herself.

Chapter 19

'What we have done for ourselves alone dies with us; what we have done for others and the world remains and is immortal.'

—Albert Pike 1899

Pedro picks up a large stone, lobs it right at the beast, smacking it square in the face. He projects his voice over the din.

"Abaddon the Destroyer. You are no king! You are a coward!" he spits.

The beast tenses.

"Look at you, you are nothing but the simplest of creatures, crawling around like the annelid that you are."

He just compared him to a leech.

The serpents surrounding him are whipped into a frenzy. He ignores them.

"Pedro, what are you doing?" Everett is panting, her energy being sapped with every swing of the axe.

He ignores her.

"You pale in the face of the one true God; you are a fool to think yourself His equal."

The tetra starts moving slowly toward him.

"Pedro, Pedro, stop!" Everett is tugging at his arm now.

The calm blooms inside him, his angst melting away leaving nothing but steely resolve.

"Miss Everett, *senhora*," he takes her by the shoulders and smiles down at her. "Have faith."

Two simple words. I understand. I dip my chin. Pedro understands.

I am Hercules.

Grandpa's poem floats through my head as I listen to Pedro hurl insults at the demon angel. Pride, greed, lust. Envy, gluttony, sloth. The battle becomes more hysterical with every affront.

Rock man is going nuclear on Jake and Achilles, ice floods my veins when it reaches down with lightning speed sweeping an arm wide, taking them both by surprise. They don't move fast enough, Jake catching the blow under the ribcage, Achilles across his broad chest.

They are thrown backwards clear across the pass, slamming into the face of the mountain. A feral caterwaul escapes my lips as they crumple to the ground. Hot tears spill down my cheeks. Pedro intensifies his taunts with even more malice in his voice.

"Your bellicosity inspires me, Abaddon. I think I will head back to the Biodome after all. I can finish what I started. Your little magic tricks bore me, you can play with your puppets all by yourself. At least your son has to courage to face me man to man. *Patético*," he finishes with disgust. Pathetic.

Pedro strikes at the very heart of the Destroyer. Taps into the deadliest of mortal sins, his pride morphing into wrath that salts the air with Sulphur and clouds the sky with billowing black thunderclouds.

Abaddon opens His cold-blooded maw wide, fangs glistening with the promise of death as venom collects in thick droplets, the earth vaporizing where they fall. He is on Pedro so fast I don't even see him move.

Pedro lifts his arm to shield himself but it's too late. The beast sinks its teeth into Pedro's forearm with so much force, his face is halfway buried in flesh. Pedro whips his arm away from his body, the creature clamped so firmly that it is an extension of his person.

"Now!" Pedro screams at me.

I am Hercules.

I grasp the axe with both hands and wind the weapon back like a baseball bat. I swing for Pedro. I swing for Jake and Achilles. I swing for Mom and Dad and Evander. I swing for mankind.

The lights flicker and the room goes dim, as though a power surge has robbed the electrical grid of power. The media agents abandon the cameras, currently positioned for a wide-angle view of the front of the room and cower in the back with the other agents.

Sandra stands her ground, isolated. She does not even care that no one comes to her aid, she'd always known they would be shrinking violets in this moment, all the bravado of the past few weeks as they prepared for this moment washed down the drain like spilled wine.

There is a stillness in her heart, a serenity. No regret, no animosity toward Maureen or the cabinet members. What will be will be.

Dr. Draeger approaches cautiously, she can feel his eyes roving over her. Intrusive, meant to frighten her. It doesn't work. He rubs his nose and purses his lips. He looks almost, impressed.

"Well, well, I see where your daughter inherited her temerity. Everett, was it? Such a shame, truly."

He pounds lightly on his chest, as though Everett's passing pains him.

A stab to the heart. He is toying with her; she must not lose control. She struggles to keep the tears from spilling over.

"You Steele women, you never know when to mind your own business."

He stares into the camera and sighs.

"And so, it falls to me, once again, to atone for the sins of the sinner."

He takes Sandra's hands in his own, the way a parent reproaches a child.

Maureen gasps, quickly followed by Gary, Henry, Edith, and others. She was wrong, they were all wrong. They just signed Sandra Steele's death warrant. He still controls the existential virus. No one moves as the righting protocol unfolds.

Heat blazes through Sandra's core, the hyperthermic shock assaulting her internal organs. She tries to wrench her hands free, Drager only tightens his grip. Her pulse accelerates, beating a dangerous tempo, black spots swim in her field of vision. 101°, 102°, her body temperature ratcheting up at an alarming rate. Once she reaches 104°, heat stroke is imminent, organ failure. Death.

Sandra stops resisting. She won't spend her last moments on Earth being afraid.

"No regrets. The truth will set you free," she whispers, her last message to the Biodome.

She smiles and closes her eyes. Waits for the end.

Draeger's eyes go impossibly wide, he starts spewing words in a language no one in the room understands.

"*Janaka? bhavAn eva kim? Naiva kila! Naiva kila!*" (Father? Is that you? No! No!)

Agents step back further, bewildered by the doctor who appears to be in a trance, his eyes a million miles away. Without warning, Draeger releases Sandra's hands, shrivels in on himself and drops to the floor.

The body collapses unceremoniously to the earth. The momentum of the blade carries the head with it, pitching it in a perfect arc. I watch it roll over and over in the air, looking at me with every spin. I feel the hate as much as I see it in those lifeless opaque eyes. I watch it hit the ground and roll out of sight.

The battle transforms. The rock giant advancing on Jake and Achilles where they lay in a heap against the mountain begins to lose its sharp edges, deliquescing with each step, molten feet sinking into the ground, anchoring it in place.

I gape, mouth hanging open, as it liquefies like a snowman in July, reduced to a giant grey puddle running off in every direction along the pass.

The serpents seem confused, as if awoken from a stupor. They lose all semblance of organization; the small, semi-transparent variety fan out, disappearing in the first burrows they find, and still more turn tail and head for the forest or scatter under the nearest cover.

The axe slides from my hand. I run to Jake and Achilles, afraid of what I will find, new tears springing to my eyes.

"Jake, please, Jake," I beg.

He moans. My heart skips a beat. He's alive.

"Jake, are you, can you—" I'm not sure what I'm asking, or maybe I'm just afraid of the answer.

He wiggles his toes for me.

"I'm okay, Evey, just need a minute or two."

I sob in relief. I reach for Achilles, place a hand on top of his big head. He responds with a twitch of his tail and a big sigh. Same message. Wounded, yes, but alive.

And then I hear Pedro. He is, laughing? Yes, laughing. Hysterically. I instinctively reach into my pockets; I have none of the florae I used on Jake's bite.

Oh no. No, no, no. I'm too late, the venom has already gotten to his brain.

I rush over to him, kneel at his side. He is lying on his back, waving his arm in the air, the bite mark swaying back and forth like a flag in the wind. I place my hand on his brow, how bad is he? I brush his hair from his face, expecting the telltale flush of fever.

"Pedro, I'm so, so sorry. Does it hurt? What can I do?"

He stops and looks at me and then, to my absolute amazement, breaks out in another fit of laughter. Is this a different kind of venom? One that steals the mind before the body? Tears are running down the side of his face from laughing so hard.

I am so discombobulated. In response to my bewilderment, he sits up, grasps his right hand firmly with his left, and pulls. I see black spots, sure I am about the faint, as his right hand and wrist pop right off, halfway to the elbow, leaving a smooth pink stump. He tosses the limb in the air.

Pedro's smile stretches across the horizon.

"Looks like I owe you one, Draeger."

The moment Draeger releases her hands, Henry rushes to Sandra's side, scooping her in his arms. The entire assembly hastens from the room leaving Dr. Vladimir Draeger in a heap on the stage.

Maureen approaches the senior agent cautiously, crouching at his side, checking for a pulse, or any signs of life. There are none. Tendrils of smoke swirl from the burnt fabric, his fine-spun suit charred along the cuffs and lapels.

She has never seen a righting protocol such as this one, she cannot imagine which expression of the existential virus the Biodome has unleashed on him. So certain that she had been wrong, that she would be responsible for Sandra Steele's demise.

She pokes at his side with a pointy black toe, feeling a paroxysm of conflicting emotions; hopeful and wretched, relieved and anxious, happy and sad. The real villain is finally vanquished, but with him, secrets she will never uncover. Who is the Master? Why was Everett Steele targeted? Where is Jacob?

On her way out of the room, she pauses briefly at the cameras, still rolling. The entire Biodome just witnessed this calamity. They've seen enough, they know the truth now. She flicks the off switch and walks out without so much as a backward glance.

Agents huddle around Sandra. Maureen switches hats to her former health promotion role. She checks Sandra's pulse rate, too high, she is suffering from acute tachycardia, but her color is returning, her body temperature regulating. Maureen is confident the worst of the crisis is over.

Sandra wrinkles her nose, swallowing over and over.

"What is in my mouth? It tastes like, like antifreeze." She winces.

"You've suffered a cytokine storm; your body threw everything it had at the attack. It will pass with time and rest," Maureen explains.

She doesn't mention the possibility of permanent organ damage. Instead, she works around the lump in her throat to formulate a collective apology.

"Sandra, we failed you."

Her eyes sweep over the agents surrounding them.

"Our own selfish need for self-preservation prevented us from coming to your aid. I am ashamed to admit that we were prepared to sacrifice you to save ourselves. No apology will ever be enough."

No one disputes, nothing but a few grumbles and nods and a lot of downturned eyes. Sandra does not appear angry or offended. She offers a meek smile.

"You heard Draeger. To be human is to be imperfect. We wage war within ourselves every day, we try to do more good than bad, more right than wrong. It was an impossible choice; I might have done the same. I knew what I signed up for and I did it willingly. But now we have the chance to want better, to do better, to be better."

The group hangs on her every word. Maureen breaks the spell with a curt order.

"You heard her! Time to dismantle this administration and set things back on the right course. Time to set the path to redemption."

Sandra is being transported to an elder care center for overnight monitoring, despite her objections. Her husband and son are on route to meet them. The mention of her family stays her protestations for the time being.

She lets her head rest against the backseat, closes her eyes. She drifts in and out of sleep almost immediately, surrounded by white noise one-minute, absolute nothingness the next, and back again. Maureen's final remark floats along with her intermittent awareness, gnawing at her conscience.

She absolved her co-agents with her poignant manifesto about the human condition, it was the right thing to do. But the war within herself rages on. Her own path to redemption will be long and arduous.

For, although she did challenge Vladimir Draeger knowingly and willingly, her heart soared with ruthless, spiteful glee when the agent finally fell. She avenged her daughter's death. What is still more good than bad?

Chapter 20

'O death, where is your victory? O death, where is your sting?'
—1 Corinthians 15:55 (ESV)

We sit around a small campfire; the exhaustion is so deep it has highjacked my bone marrow. Pedro is explaining how he came to be one-handed, his confrontation with Draeger in the Ceará, how he knew Draeger was not who he claimed to be when he survived the survivable, even before he found Dr. Castillo's hidden file.

How he counted on Abaddon being unaware of his newly acquired debility. How he put two and two together, drawing the parallels to our time in the Android. He manipulated his snake army the same way he controlled his clones.

Of course, now that he says it, I can see how Abaddon deployed the snakes. Pedro admits the freakish rock monster being under the tetra's command was pure conjecture, he could only reason that there was no other explanation.

The prosthetic limb is back in place. Other than the twin puncture marks from the bite, Pedro is totally unscathed. Jake is a little worse for wear, stiff, his articulations arthritic. He needs time, but he will make a full recovery.

Achilles has a bad limp on the back leg but no visible sign of damage. He's weight-bearing, so Jake is fairly certain it's a soft tissue injury. We clean and inspect the bloody fur on his left flank, thankfully more of a superficial scrape than a laceration.

Three miracles. Well four, if you count the fact that I came out this in one piece.

I don't remember falling asleep, but the next thing I know, brilliant rays of sunshine streak the sky from the east. Sunshine! It's been so long, I'd almost forgotten how magnificent it feels to be washed in the yellow glow, to behold the perfect, depthless cerulean sky. The infernal heat and humidity that has been sapping our strength and destroying the garden plant by plant, animal by animal, is dissipating.

I breathe in deep, my lungs rejoicing in air so pure and fresh, it's intoxicating. Birds, I hear birds singing and chirping in the morning radiance, flowers unfurling on stems that have sprung back to life. All the trials and tribulations of the last week are fading to grey, losing their hold on me as I witness the rebirth of the garden.

We spend the morning exploring, rediscovering the enchantment. I do have one burning need, and it is denied to me. I need to see it one last time. I know where the tetra fell, and yet the body is nowhere to be found. I watched as the head spun through the air, watched it land, watched it roll into the side of the mountain. I will never forget those nubilous eyes, imprecating me, even in death. It too, vanished into thin air.

I can't dwell on it, I won't dampen the little spring in Jake's walk, the brilliant smile on Pedro's face.

Jake leads the way, retracing our steps, Achilles pads alongside him, his left hip still tender. We begin the journey back through the forest. The scars are everywhere; the ravages of the pestilence abound; the waterlogged soil carries with it the underlying smell of decay that fills my nostrils.

Death is everywhere, from the tiniest forest dormouse to the most majestic 12-point elk. If some small part of me wanted to believe it was all a bad dream, I no longer harbor any such illusion.

Jake is like a homing pigeon; he walks a straight path back to our camp and announces we will rest here for tonight. Although our stay in this clearing was brief, the familiarity of the camp; the tree root shelter, the fire pit, the split log bench, provides a little much-needed sanguinity.

Jake makes short work of starting a fire while Pedro and I scour the vicinity for a late dinner. Achilles is gone and back before we sit around the flames, his dietary needs met for the night.

"We'll set out at first light," Jake announces. "We should reach the old creek by mid-day."

I fill in more blanks for Pedro. The volcano, the dams, the tree, our tree. Our home.

"*Si*, I remember the tree," Pedro states quietly. "It was a holy place."

Jake looks up in surprise. Now I have to fill in the blanks for him too.

"It was a long time ago. We were at the annual conference, that's where Pedro and I first met. We both saw the tetra, er' Abaddon I guess, crawl inside the Biodome, right into the mouth of the Android. We needed to compare notes, suss each other out. It was during that second meeting that we were kind of, swept up on the wind and deposited in the garden. We found the tree and the—"

I can't finish. Jake senses my discomfort. Pedro and I exchange a knowing look.

"What? What are you two not telling me?"

Mild annoyance is laminated over frustration in his tone.

"It's when we found a bloody fleece. Freshly washed and drying out behind the tree," I say without making eye contact.

"No one's judging," I add desperately.

"Evey," his eyes plead with me. This is the unfinished conversation from our time with the Empress. Looks like we can't avoid it now.

"That was the day of the storm, the omen. The day the tetra returned to the Biodome. That hide was left on my doorstep. To taunt me, to remind me there was nothing I could do to stop him this time."

I didn't realize how much I needed to be mollified until this moment. I am ashamed, was there a sliver of doubt in my heart? I didn't think so but now I'm not so sure. As if Pedro reads my mind, he interjects on my behalf.

"*Senhor*, Miss Everett never doubted you. It was I who questioned the origin of the fleece. *Desculpa Jacó*, I am sorry. Now that I know you, I feel foolish for my ambiguity," he wrings his hands.

Jake looks relieved.

"No worries, Pedro. I get it. I mean, it was pretty sickening and it was on my doorstep. But I wouldn't, couldn't, take a life."

"*Si*, I see that now," Pedro confesses.

Jake lets us off the hook by changing the subject, striking up one of our old games of *name that constellation*. Big mistake. Pedro is like a walking, talking astrophysicist, pointing out one zodiac sign after another, identifying other planets and even a black hole. We finish the game in a fit of warm laughter crowning Pedro the undisputed champion. And then Pedro gets very serious.

"*Meus amigos*, I am blessed. To bear witness to this consecrated land. To defend it against evil. To know I leave it in good hands."

Jake and I both sit up straighter now, my brain working out a remonstration. I don't get the chance.

"I must return. There is much work to do in the Biodome. I must ensure the existential virus is unhindered. And," he looks at our intertwined hands, "there is someone, I left behind. Things I've left undone."

A faint blush colors his cheeks.

I understand. I don't try to convince him to stay, it is his choice and I have to respect his wishes. Jake is quiet beside me; I surmise he's thinking the very same.

"Well, not tonight, deal?" Jake tries to keep it light. Pedro agrees.

"Pedro," I too, am serious now. "Could I ask a favor? When you return, I mean?"

He looks at me quizzically, but when he sees the tears welling in my eyes, he understands how much this means to me. He doesn't even ask me what I need from him.

"Of course, *senhora*, whatever it is, I will see to it. My promise to you."

A few hours later, Gordon and Evander Steele maintain their vigilance by Sandra's bedside as she awakens. Worry is painted all over Gordon's face while Evander trips over his own words with excitement.

"Mom! Mom, you're the talk of the Biodome. Everyone is calling you a hero. My mom, Super Sandra, woman of *steel*," he laughs. "Get it? Sandra Steele, made of steel?"

Sandra groans. Gordon chuckles.

"What did you expect, honey? You single-handedly disgraced Vladimir Draeger, exposed him for the despot he is and saved us all from going the way of the ancients. We were prepared to accept a return to the tyranny of man. You redeemed us."

There's that word again. And that same pang of contrition. She's no hero, she's just a heartbroken mother. She has yet to forgive herself for her ignominious motives. She doubts she ever will.

"Look guys, no more super steel, or super mom, or whatever, okay?" she beseeches. "I just want to go home."

A quiet knock at the door has them all turning toward the sound. A very weary Maureen Domanso steps into the room, looking a bit like a lost puppy. Her eyes land on Evander and Sandra knows something has broken inside her.

"I apologize for the interruption," she begins.

Sandra waves an arm in the air.

"It's fine Maureen. This is my husband Gordon and my son Evander."

Gordon stands and shakes her hand gently. She gives him a slight smile. Evander is next, standing a few inches shorter than Maureen in her customary pump heels. The boy emulates his father, extending his hand. This time Maureen wraps both her hands around his and holds on. She studies his face with melancholy eyes. Sandra knows she is thinking of her own son. Two mothers, one heart.

"You are what? 15?" she asks with genuine interest.

"Yes, ma'am," Evander is a bit skittish with the woman's intensity.

"Ah then, only a couple of years away from your initiation. No matter what you choose, no matter how you serve the Biodome, your mother and father will be so proud. You are cherished all the days of your life."

She lays a hand on his cheek, Evander stands frozen, eyes like saucers.

Maureen pulls away, embarrassed. She brushes her eyes and heaves a giant sigh. Gordon gives Sandra a bewildered look, only Sandra knows those words were intended for her own son, words left unspoken. Regret she will carry with her for the rest of her days.

"Gord, could you take Ev for a bite to eat down in the cafeteria? You two must be famished, I'll bet you've been sitting here for hours."

When Gordon raises his eyebrows, she adds, "It's not like I'm going anywhere!"

Her husband concedes with a casual shrug.

"Well, what do you say Ev? I think your mom is trying to get rid of us."

"Maureen and I just have a little, business, to finish up is all. I'll be right here; we'll all be able to speak with the health agent. I don't want to waste any more Biodome resources, we are all going home. Together. Today."

"Okay, Mom, you win," Evander turns to his father.

"She's back," he says, lifting both hands in surrender.

With the boys gone for some late lunch, Sandra turns her head toward Maureen, intent on finishing their earlier conversation. She must have fallen asleep in the back of the car, every cell in her body sapped of strength from the overheating. She can keep up now. She's stronger, certainly nowhere near 100% but she'll keep that little titbit close to the vest.

"You know, they are right to be worried about you," Maureen starts up the new discourse. "You were on the edge of irreversible injury."

"Yes, well, I didn't go over that edge, did I? The Biodome protected me in the end. That was no righting protocol, that was, him. I don't know how to explain it, but he was doing it, not with the existential virus, it was something else."

Maureen is quiet, considering her statement. She looks out the window, staring into the distance at nothing in particular. Her eyes return to Sandra.

"I believe you. Especially now."

"What do you mean?"

"Once I got you settled here, I returned to retrieve the body. I was going to dispose of it at the crematorium, we talked about this in the car?" She probes for Sandra's recognition.

Sandra nods, yes, she remembers that part from the car ride. They had agreed it would be better to extirpate Dr. Draeger's remains as swiftly, and quietly, as possible. No fanfare, not even a funeral. It seemed cold, even for him, but they both wanted to close this bleak chapter in the New Order and begin making reparations.

"Have you changed your mind now that you've had some time to process? I suppose, that's understandable, you did serve the man quite a long time after all," she exhales, relenting. "I won't attend the funeral, but I will respect your need for closure."

Maureen rounds on her with the same look she had when Sandra had slapped her. The memory of that day is still vivid in her mind. Not one of her finest moments.

"No," is all she says, bringing her emotions under cool control.

She has the look of defeat.

Sandra is perplexed. She waits for Maureen to explain.

"The room was still locked when I returned, I was the only key holder. Besides, there was no one, I mean no one, left in that building. Everyone had scattered like scared rabbits."

She has a vague recollection of the chaos that followed Draeger's fall. The mad rush for the door. She can hear Maureen swallow.

"When I opened the door, the smell hit me like a ton of bricks."

"Well, it was a deadly correction, and it happened so fast, the tissue necrosis from the infection would have been severe," Sandra reasons.

"Not that kind of smell."

"Oh, I just assumed—" she begins, but Maureen waves her off.

"It's logical conjecture. But no, this was a very distinct stench. It was irrefutable. It was Sulphur."

"Sulphur? Now where in the Biodome would that come from?" Sandra wonders out loud.

Maureen is pale as death, with a tone as bleached as her complexion.

"No," she repeats cogently. "That smell was not from the Biodome. There was a chasm, in the center of the stage, right where the lectern was supposed to be. It was smoldering, it was red hot. That, that, pit, it was breathing fire and brimstone," Maureen shivers as she recounts.

Sandra forgets to blink as she hangs on her every word.

"I swear every molecule of oxygen in that room was displaced. It was impossible to breathe."

"Oh my, and you were all alone. Moving the body under those conditions must have been incredibly strenuous. I am sorry I couldn't help," Sandra offers as an apology.

"Oh, it was no bother at all," Maureen chuckles at Sandra's confusion.

"You see, there was no body. It was already gone."

Chinda grunts under the weight of the body slung over her tiny shoulders. When the Master sent her on this errand, He failed to mention that Vlad would be completely incapacitated. Sometimes He overestimates her strength.

Time is of the essence; the Master must close the rift before it is discovered. Chinda doubts any sane human would explore the chasm, but she keeps her opinion to herself. She ducks back down the void without incident. Vlad owes her for this one.

She doubles back through the passageway, her charge limp as a noodle, his chin and arms slapping at her backside as she maneuvers the rough terrain. The master was not being facetious when He instructed her to make haste; the ceiling of the tunnel rumbles behind her, caving in on itself, matching her step for step.

"*Lā shǐ*," she curses in her mother tongue. "Not even one inch."

She chokes on clouds of dust, her eyes gritty, watering involuntarily. A litany of profanities ricochet off the stone walls as she presses on, somehow making the journey more bearable.

Chinda finally steps through the outer rim, the lip of the shaft closing at her heels like a giant maw. Back in the palace, in the dungeons. She drops one last silent curse as she makes for the spiraling staircase and begins her ascent.

Chapter 21

'There's no place like home.'
—Dorothy (Judy Garland) The Wizard of Oz, 1939

Chinda places him gently down on the bed, soot blemishing the red satin pillowcase. Vlad lay still as death, his leaden skin bleeding into his grey suit. Chinda snaps to attention when she hears the echo of footsteps coming down the polished marble hallway toward the bedroom.

She needs no visual confirmation; there is only one who walks with such conviction. He does not slow a beat, she opens and holds the door at just the right moment, the ornate black robe flourishing in his wake. His silken mane settles about his shoulders as his heavy boots come to an abrupt stop at the bed's edge. Chinda drops to one knee behind him and bows deep. He doesn't turn.

"At ease child."

"My Lord," she stands.

"Complications?" he asks simply.

"None, my Lord."

"Very well."

The Master's version of thanks.

The connection was severed along with his serpent head. He sets about the task of re-establishing it. He grasps Vladimir's hands with heavily jeweled fingers, imbuing his son with his life force. Vladimir gasps and bolts upright, esurient lungs gulping down mouthfuls of air. He is fanatical, eyes darting around the room as the mental fog lifts.

"Father," he utters, dipping his chin and making for his knees.

He scrambles onto the floor and assumes the correct position.

"Rise, son. We have much to discuss."

Draeger obeys, noticing Chinda in the corner of the room for the first time. Father answers his unasked question.

"Yes, she is the paladin of your mortal form. And to your next query, it was necessary to pierce the veil briefly to reclaim your form. There was no time for circumspection."

Draeger is astonished. Father has only breached the boundary a handful of times, and then only to personally welcome his most highly coveted VIPs. Genghis Khan, Ivan the Terrible, and Vlad the Impaler all come to mind and then more recently, Father created a special portal for those two genocidal heretics Draeger liked to tease with their matching toothbrush moustaches and rhythming surnames. Chinda clears her throat more garishly than necessary, cuing Draeger to hearken back to the present.

"Father, you were, gone, completely," he fumbles.

"It is true, I cannot assume the reptilian configuration, not presently."

He does not elaborate, as if this information were frivolous.

"But then, Father, all is lost. You can never return to the Biodome. And I, the entire Biodome watched me die. I could not possibly go back now."

Draeger feels his composure slipping.

Father raises a brow.

"Really now, such an improvident perspective. I had not thought you to be so myopic," Father submits the barbed reproach.

He takes Draeger's chin in his hand, lifting it to the wall torch burning brightly near the bed, turning his face to the left, then to the right.

"Not to worry, you will remain as alluring as ever, as is befitting your illustrious genealogy."

Draeger feels the blood rush to his head as Father's intendment sinks in. He is formulating a coherent counterargument when he is interrupted by a knock at the bedroom door. The blood reverses course, draining his face of all color with Father's final words on the subject.

"Ah, and here is the good doctor now."

Pedro flinches when the hypodermic syringe breaks the skin and slides into the ventrogluteal muscle.

"*Ai!*" he croaks, shifting away from the assault.

"Pedro!" a cheery female voice twitters as she presses the plunger on the needle into his hip.

He slides to the opposite edge of the bed to no avail. The female agent is adept at her task.

"Oh, this is just diphenhydramine, it's to help control the inflammation and should help with the itching. Now that you are awake and all. You gave everyone quite a scare. I'd better page Dr. O'Mara, she will be so pleased."

As if her words activate the pruritis, Pedro lifts his left hand to his neck where the first prickle demands attention. His fingers are fat as overstuffed sausages, his hand puffy and disfigured with purple and yellowing welts crawling one over the other. He snorts at the sight of it, fumbling for his neck. It's like trying to scratch while wearing boxing gloves.

"*Senhora, é ruim?*" he enunciates in his native tongue.

It takes him a second, the blank stare from the health agent alerting him to his mistake.

"I look, bad?" his brain is sluggish, slow to translate the question.

His pharynx and vocal cords feel as though they've been subjected to a cheese grater. He examines the hand in front of his face, oddly fascinated with his body's immunologic response to the bees. The health agent winces before responding, reaching for a handheld mirror in a drawer on her medical cart.

"It was much worse actually; the swelling and redness have settled down. Quite a lot. The bruising is starting to fade. But you still look—" she hesitates, unsure of the appropriate adjective.

She settles on, "aggrieved."

She holds the mirror in front of his face. He blinks twice. Barely recognizable, even to himself. There is not one inch of flesh spared. Not even his ears. He bursts out laughing at his knobby reflection, his core muscles cramping in protest. The health agent springs to his bedside.

"Shhh, Pedro, you are weak. You need to rest. Now that you are awake, I expect your visitors will be back. Except—" her demeanor changes, solemnity creeping in.

"Wait, visitors? What visitors *senhora*?"

Pedro lives on the other side of the Biodome, he has no family or colleagues here, and his only friend, well two friends actually, will not be visiting, that is a certainty.

"Well, for one, Maureen Domanso has been by to see you a number of times now. She is quite concerned for your welfare. Sandra Steele has been by as well. And then, well, Dr. Draeger won't be back."

Pedro's ears hone in on that last one like an antenna.

"Dr. Draeger, he was here?" Pedro's skin crawls when the name passes over his tongue.

"Not exactly, but he did call. With specific instructions that he was to be notified the moment you awakened. But of course, that is no longer pertinent."

She shuffles uncomfortably from foot to foot.

"I do not understand, *senhora*, why has Dr. Draeger suddenly lost interest in my case?"

Pedro can't imagine Draeger letting bygones be bygones. After all, the doctor's intent was not to injure or maim, Draeger threw him in that bee cage to silence him. Permanently. There has to be more to this story.

The health agent's eyes dart around the room, her voice dropping to a feathery whisper. She trips over her speech, seemingly unable to formulate the words. Pedro is growing impatient.

"What is it," he scans her agent badge, clipped to the breast pocket of her pink scrubs for a name. "Miss Krista, what is it?" he pleads.

She clears her throat and quells her anxiety.

"Pedro, Dr. Draeger is dead."

Krista's words hang in the air between them. Pedro is still processing the news when Dr. O'Mara ploughs into the room like a bull in a fine china shop, her bifocals askew on her petite face, half dangling from the brightly beaded lanyard attached to the eyeglasses.

Her arms are overflowing with files, patient records sticking out of the manilla folders at all angles, her ash grey hair slipping in random wisps from a messy bun on top of her head. There is a coffee stain on the front of her billowing lab coat and ink leaking onto the pocket from the blue pen poking out.

The lines around her mouth and the crow's feet around the eyes run deep, a face accustomed to smiling. She discards the files in a sloppy pile on the counter behind the bed like they are nothing more than old newsprint and rushes to his side.

Exactly what he would have done.

"Pedro, my dear boy! It is true then!"

Warm, open, genuine. Exactly how he would have said it.

She pushes the glasses too far up the bridge of her nose absentmindedly as she takes his vitals, checks his chart, and whips the pen out of her pocket to take notes, all at the same time.

Exactly the same. Right down to the glasses.

Pedro stares at the doctor, his heart soring. He, she, six feet, five feet, blue eyes, brown eyes, golden, porcelain. They couldn't be more physically contrastive. And yet. She is disorganized. She is disheveled. She is distractible. She is brilliance hidden in plain sight.

She brings Dr. Castillo back to life in vivid color; all the heartwarming memories buried deep under the guilt and petulance come flooding in like a tidal wave.

Pedro casts his eyes out the window into the clear, endless sky.

"*Não diga mais nada, meu Senhor,* say no more, my Lord."

"Pedro, is everything alright? You look like you've seen a ghost child!"

Dr. O'Mara's huge owl eyes blink just inches from his nose. Even her wizened scent is reminiscent of his old mentor.

"Not a ghost *doutor*, a gift."

Krista and Dr. O'Mara exchange a glance.

"Are you sure you're okay, Pedro?"

"*Si*, I am better than I've been in a very long time."

A look of surprise crosses the doctor's face, the conversation all but forgotten. She shuffles to the other side of the bed and leans into him, tilting her head like a curious dog. Pedro raises his right arm to inspect the source of her concern; surely, they all know by now that the arm is prosthetic.

"Now, how do you suppose those got to be here? I personally catalogued your injuries; the artificial limb was completely unblemished. And besides, these do not look like anything a bee could produce, no matter how angry."

Pedro brings the arm to eye level, his own curiosity peaked. Two identical clefts partway up the forearm, with a depression in between them. For the briefest instant, he sees Him, feels Him, latched on, biting down with a ferocity that makes his spine tingle. A small price to pay for victory. A memento, a reminder, a permanent link. To the Beginning, to them.

"I have no idea, Dr. O'Mara. But I assure you, it causes me no pain. None whatsoever."

I know he's gone before I open my eyes. His absence is as manifest as the warm sun banking the horizon to the east. I peer through my lashes. Jake is watching me, the curve of a smile forming, one arm pillowing his head, his free hand playing with my poor excuse for a ponytail.

Achilles is splayed out at our feet. He lifts his head just enough to tell me he knows I am awake and, deciding he's not quite ready for the day, plops his head back down. I know the feeling. Every muscle in my body is screaming for more sleep. But I need to know.

"Did you see, I mean, were you awake when, when he left?"

What I really want to ask is if he made it back to the Biodome safely. That my friend is alright.

Jake senses my equivocation.

"Pedro is home, Evey. He is going to be just fine."

He says it with such conviction, I have to believe it to be true. I need it to be true. Jake brushes his thumb on my forehead.

"You know, frown lines turn into permanent wrinkles," he points out in jest. But I smooth out my face anyway, just in case.

Jake prepares manioc over the fire, softening the starchy root for us while I clean the açai berries I've collected in my pockets. After we've eaten our fill and Achilles returns satiated from his morning hunt, Jake is already growing restless.

I sigh, knowing today is going to be another day of relentless trekking, and with it, more aches and cramps and sore feet. But I also know how much Jake needs to go home, to assess the damage, to determine if there is still hope for the garden. I need to be stoic, for him.

We break from the forest into a sun-filled sky and a soft breeze that sweeps across my damp face. I scan the skyline and my stomach twists. Everything is as it was; the bed of ugly grey lava runs up to the opposite side of the dry stream bed and back as far as the eye can see.

I don't know what I was expecting. That somehow it would all disappear with the tetra? I am reproving myself for the gormless idealism when Jake dashes into the stream bed, a million-watt smile on his face.

"Evey, the stones are wet!"

He breaks out into a sprint up the middle of the channel, Achilles right beside him, his paws throwing spots of mud onto his perfectly white underside. I lag some distance behind them.

"Jake, wait up!" I call to him.

He slows, marginally, but I don't lose sight of them. When I catch up, they are standing at the base of the monumental dam. Twelve feet thick and ten high, it should be impenetrable, unbreachable. Against all odds, a tiny rivulet of life-giving water has battered its way through the stone and trees and mud chinking.

I watch the droplets collect at the hard-won opening, meander down the face of the dam and fall onto the shiny stones below, running along the middle of the canal, already almost an inch deep.

The structure is now destabilized, it takes Jake no time at all to hammer at the crack until a waterfall gushes through the opening and the stream is revived. We laugh like fools, taking turns under the spray, the sweat and grime and filth carried away on the rising watercourse.

Flashes of silver sparkle in the air when the sun catches minnows as they fall over the edge and scurry downstream. Achilles splashes in after them, his muzzle fully immersed as he tries desperately to capture them as they make their escape. It is a small victory in the face of the moldy grey landscape before us but I'll take it.

The shower is salubrious, I feel more refreshed than I've felt in days, maybe even weeks. I'm practically skipping, that is until Jake starts up the blanket of insipid lava. I stop. Why spoil the moment?

"Jake, maybe we should stay on the, uhm, green side? I mean, what is there to see that way? It's just going to be more of the same."

I try to be delicate while pointing out the obvious. It's drab and somber as far as the eye can see. Jake is introspective, a slight shake of his head the only sign that he's heard me. He doesn't turn around, he stands poised on the balls of his feet, looking, or maybe listening.

"Do you hear it?"

So, listening then.

I don't hear anything except the wind rustling through the trees at my back. Achilles points his ears up and forward, in the same direction. His body language tells me that whatever it is they've descried, it is not threatening.

"Ugh, okay you two, what gives? I don't hear anything!"

"Music," he says. "Singing."

He picks up a jog. I have no choice but to follow.

We are about fifty feet up the slope and there it is. It's carried on the wind, reminding me instantly of the story of Odysseus from classic literature, the lure of the muses. Seductive, enchanting, a harmony of soft voices melding together. It is a hymn in Allegro with flawless pitch, my heart beating in synchrony with the tempo.

It grows stronger the farther up the plume of lava we travel, beckoning us. It feels surreal, I wonder if it's all a dream. Jake slows and then stops altogether. I am right behind him, joining him at his side.

The voices reach a crescendo and then, one by one, they fall away, leaving a silence and a stillness that defies gravity. The source of the music stares back at us. The Tree of Life, our tree, already twelve inches high, sprouting through the lava. Rich. Green. Strong. Alive. And at its base, a halo of life radiates around the tree, devouring death. We are home.

Chapter 22

'Now faith is the assurance of things hoped for, the conviction of things not seen.'

—Hebrews 11:1 (ESV)

Sandra is puttering around the kitchen in her Sunday lounge wear; matching navy-blue joggers and hoodie with her department acronym in bold letters on the back, fake fur-lined slippers, her hair trapped in a pink scrunchie on top of her head.

She feels so, weekend Everett, the thought brings a smile to her lips and a pang to her heart. After all the notoriety of late, she is happy to be in her safe space, away from all the unwanted attention.

She's just finished organizing the lazy Suzan and is about to tackle the refrigerator when the doorbell sounds. Evander bounces down the stairs at breakneck speed, making her cringe.

"Got it!" he races to the door. "That'll be Angelo, we're going to shoot some hoops before dinner."

Gordon pokes his head out from the basement door. He's been down there for hours working on his latest refinishing project, a fabulous old rocking chair that will go great out on the porch.

"Did I hear company?" he asks moving to the kitchen.

"Just Angelo from next door, Gord. You look thirsty, lemonade?"

Without affirming, he reaches into the cupboard for a glass. They both pause when they catch sight of Evander coming back down the hallway toward them. As he approaches, Sandra's stomach drops at his bollixed expression.

"Mom," he starts slowly. "There's someone here who says he needs to talk to you."

"Okay, Ev, but why does your face say there's a mythical beast at the front door?" she laughs at her own joke.

Evander does not reciprocate. That sinking feeling returns. Sandra leads, Gordon and Evander in tow.

She appreciates her son's misgivings the second she sees the boy on the porch. Although he has convalesced considerably since she last saw him, Pedro Ramón's injuries are nevertheless shocking.

His skin is a spectacular array of greens and yellows, peppered with scabs and residual inflammation that renders his complexion blotchy and uneven.

Had she not known what happened to this poor boy, she would assume he had been dealt a serious righting protocol for some unspeakable transgression, which is exactly what Evander must be thinking.

"It's okay, Ev," she says in a calm voice, never taking her eyes off Pedro. "This is not what you think."

Evander looks to his father for assurance, but her husband is oblivious, unsure of what to do or say. She can feel him wound tight as a spring behind her, ready to lunge.

"Gord, I know him. He is, was, Everett's friend. And I know what you're both thinking, but this is not the work of the existential virus."

She doesn't elaborate.

"Pedro. I apologize for the discourtesy. Please, come in."

She moves to the side, sweeping her husband and son out of the way.

"*Obrigato senhora*," Pedro reaches for his face self-consciously.

"I am, Kafkaesque, even to my own eyes, it is understandable."

His self-deprecation dissipates the tension. He walks over the threshold into the foyer, visibly nervous.

"You are looking much better," Sandra offers truthfully. "Give it another week or so and you'll be good as new."

"*Si*, I feel a little better each day, *senhora*."

"So then, what *did* happen to you, dude?" Evander is still dubious.

"Evander!" Sandra and Gordon admonish in unison. Pedro chuckles.

"It is no trouble," he turns his gaze to the teen. "Bees, 2511 to be exact. It was a most unfortunate, mishap," he hesitates on the last word.

Evander's eyes go wide as saucers, his misanthropy withering like a desert flower.

"Holy smokes, that's rough. Sorry for the attitude man," the apology is sincere.

Just then Evander notices the incongruity of Pedro's right hand. This time his stupefaction wins out over his manners, and he stares. Pedro lifts the sleeve of his camel-colored cable knit sweater and extends his arm out. Two parallel holes, one inch apart, between his wrist and elbow. The only disfigurement of the limb.

"What the—" Gordon doesn't finish.

Pedro removes the prosthetic arm and waves his stump in the air.

"It seems bees have a very discerning palate. They care not for the taste of metal and latex."

"Oh, my goodness," Sandra gasps. "It looks so real."

She is horrified by what she's said and quickly adds, "Oh dear child, you've suffered more misfortune than most endure in a lifetime."

She winces at the pity dripping in her words.

Pedro shakes his head.

"No *senhora*, your dysphoria is misplaced. I am perhaps the luckiest person in the entire Biodome. Please listen to what I am about to tell you. Have faith."

He refastens the prosthetic limb and then takes a deep breath.

"Miss Everett has asked me to come."

He waits.

Evander takes a step back. Gordon reaches for his arm to steady both of them. Sandra stands still as stone, her eyes locked on Pedro. She slowly begins to shake her head.

"What, what are you talking about? Everett has been, gone for months now. She is deceased Pedro."

She says the last sentence through clenched teeth.

"Gone, yes, *senhora*. But not deceased."

Evander gasps audibly and turns to run from the foyer. Pedro stops him in his tracks.

"In her bedroom, upstairs, the third door on the right. There is a nightstand beside the window, and in the top drawer she keeps her socks. Under the pink slipper socks at the back of the drawer, on the left side, there is a silver box."

No one objects so he presses on.

"It was given to her by her grandmother on her 14th birthday. Inside that box, Everett has stored three items. Will you retrieve it? Please, do not open the box."

Evander turns around, glaring at Pedro.

"How, how do you know this stuff? Where her room is? Where she keeps her socks? Her mementos? Is this some kind of parlor trick? Cause it's not funny."

He's lost all pretense of civility, he is trembling, tears pooling in the corners of his eyes.

"No *senhor*, she told me," he says simply, not reacting to the hostility.

Sandra is reeling. Part of her always wondered, always knew, on some level. Everett did not fall victim to a righting protocol that fated day. She did not die in her bed.

Snippets of her confrontation with Maureen Domanso in the abattoir, *it's him isn't it, Dr. Draeger has Everett.* Domanso's confession, her own son's mysterious disappearance.

"Evander, stop," her tone brooks no argument.

Gordon sidles up to his son and rubs his hands in circles on his back in a calming gesture.

She pivots and heads straight for the stairs. No one speaks.

Everett's door is slightly ajar. Sandra opens it to find Minx sprawled out over her bed, the tip of his tail twitching at the sight of her.

She runs her hand the length of the cat's outstretched body, summoning the courage to open the nightstand drawer two feet away, praying there is a silver box under pink socks. Hope courses through her veins, in all its paradoxical glory. Exhilarating and heartrending. Merciful and cruel.

Evander and Gordon are standing in the doorway now, watching, waiting. Minx senses the change in the air and meows, jumps from the bed and scurries away out the door. With nothing left to distract her, Sandra approaches the nightstand and gently pulls the drawer outward.

All three hold their collective breath as she rummages to the back, her hand going left. Her heart leaps when she eyes the pink socks. She handles them like a landmine, lifting them from their resting place. A sharp intake of air fills her lungs when the top of a silver box is exposed.

Sandra looks to her husband and son, tears streaming down her cheeks, and nods once.

The three walk back to the foyer, Sandra in front, holding the box with the care of a newborn child. She presents it to Pedro, her hand shaking, the pretty silver bow affixed to the lid shimmering in the light.

"Maybe we could sit in the family room for this?" Gordon suggests.

Sandra is spellbound. She nods and they make their way down the hallway. She looks over her shoulder, fearing if she takes her eyes off the boy, he might vanish, and she will never know. And that would eat away at her from the inside out for the rest of her life.

Mother, Father, and Son sit like ducks in a row on the edge of the sofa, Pedro taking the wing chair across from them. He opens the box gingerly and smiles when he looks inside.

"*Si*, exactly as Miss Everett instructed," more to himself than his audience.

"*Senhor Steele*," he starts. "Everett's message to you: If you look hard enough, you will find the needle in the haystack. And if you cannot, you can always mow the lawn."

Pedro shrugs, clearly not understanding, "She said you would know what this means."

He retrieves a tiny plastic unicorn from the box and hands it to Gordon Steele. The older man stares at his daughter's childhood toy, she carried it with her everywhere for the longest time, the paint worn away where her little fingers held the figurine. The day she lost it in the backyard, his belly laughs when she turned puppy dog eyes on him in confusion after his father's use of the ancient idiom from the porch where he watched her searching frantically.

"Gord, does this mean anything to you?" Sandra probes.

She was not part of this memory; it is his and his alone.

"It means everything to me."

He retreats into himself, lost in thought, drowning in memories.

Sandra turns her attention back to the box. Pedro addresses Evander now.

"Your sister wanted me to tell you how proud she is. She wanted me to say just this: Boundless day, endless night. And for you, infinite possibility."

He reaches into the box and pulls out a small silver lemniscate on a matching chain.

"She had this made for your birthday."

Evander takes the proffered piece of jewelry, turning it over in his hands. He too, absorbed in a private remembrance. After a moment, Sandra helps him with the clasp and the chain is slung around his neck, the lemniscate nestled in between his collarbones. Her son weeps silently.

Pedro faces Sandra.

"Miss Everett wants, needs you to know that leaving was her choice for reasons that will remain her own. She is well, and whole, and happy. She wants you to know the hyacinths grow wild where she is, the fragrance is often carried on the breeze, making her think of you."

A reference to Sandra's favorite flower, her favorite scent.

"She wants you all to know she loves you very much. Do not feel sorrow, but rather rejoice. This is her destiny. This is her purpose."

Pedro retrieves a glossy speckled river stone from the box and places it in Sandra's hand.

"Hold this stone when you want to be near your daughter, for this is where you will find her. She will feel you and says, if you open your heart, you will feel her as well."

The tears fall like rain. Sandra holds the stone as if her life depends on it. And in a way, it does. She cannot go on like this, the world losing a little more color every day, little pieces of her falling away bit by bit. For the first time since Everett's passing, no, not passing, she's simply moved on, she has hope that she might just find redemption after all.

"Will she ever come back?" Sandra shifts back to Pedro.

He shakes his head ruefully.

"Is she all alone, there, wherever she is?"

Pedro is unsure how to respond, he hesitates. That's all the answer Sandra needs.

"Jacob," she murmurs.

A flash of surprise in the boy's eyes, there and gone. But enough.

"Does Maureen know?"

Pedro is truly puzzled now.

"*Senhora*? Maureen?"

"Maureen Domanso. Jacob's mother," Sandra clarifies.

He vacillates. Sandra senses he is about to repudiate her supposition.

"Please, Pedro. There is no point in trying to deny it. Wherever they are, Jacob and Everett are together."

Pedro looks defeated and after a few silent seconds tick by, finally capitulates.

"*Si*, this is true. But *Senhor* Jacó—" he fumbles, trying to find the right words.

He scrunches up his face as if it pains him to continue.

"He said his *mãe,* his mother that is, would not care to learn of his fate, has little to no concern for his welfare, and wouldn't even listen to me if I tried to explain. And his papa, well, he said his papa always follows her lead, he will just stand behind her, in her shadow."

Sandra shakes her head. The old Maureen Domanso, maybe. But not now, not this enlightened, compassionate Maureen Domanso. The child will never know the truth. That his mother has been searching for him, that she gave up everything to find him, that she betrayed Draeger for him. That she changed for him. That she found redemption. Too little too late.

"Will you, can you, see them, again? If you want to?"

The barely coherent question comes from Evander.

"I honestly do not know," Pedro looks out the window, a dreamy smile lifts the corners of his mouth. "It is not up to me. I can only hope, one day."

Evander looks puzzled, he furrows his brow and opens his mouth to interject when Pedro shifts his focus back to the family, staying his question. Sandra watches this boy, so wise beyond his years, learned in a way that transcends mundane edification.

His final words to the Steeles' will remain with Sandra for the rest of her days and she is eternally grateful to the young man.

"Have faith."

She churns the stone between her fingers in a slow, soothing pattern, over and over and over. It brings with it a serenity she'd thought was lost forever. Sandra is finally free.

Chapter 23

'One of the artifices of Satan is, to induce men to believe that he does not exist.'
—John Wilkinson, Quakerism Examined (1836)

Vlad stands in front of the ornate cheval mirror, tilting it to catch his reflection in the unsteady light cast from the open flame. The last of the bandages fall at his feet. Father chose a renowned forensic facial reconstruction surgeon who moonlighted for many a criminal syndicate in his hay day.

He had assured Vlad that the scalpel was an extension of the man's hand, his skill with the blade unmatched. As he studies his new face, he finds Father's accolades were warranted after all. An elegant aquiline nose lends him a certain neoteric sophistication while his profile is transformed with deftly placed submalar implants.

The oculoplastic reconstruction is dramatic, he stares at himself through dangerous and seductive fox eyes. The widow's peak is a nice touch, unleashing his inner Dracula. Father was gracious in granting his request to maintain his congenital coloring. He anchors himself to his lustrous black hair and deep brown eyes, finding solace in these remnants of who he is.

He clears his throat and introduces himself in the accent he has adopted as part of his new persona, a distinguished parlance in the tradition of the ancient French nobility.

"It is a pleasure to make your acquaintance. Geoffroi de Kigal, *agent extraordinaire,* at your service."

He had fun coming up with the name. A homage to a favorite period in human history where one Geoffroi de Charny stands out, a famous 14th-century knight who died defending his king on the battlefield. He was the embodiment of loyalty and gallantry, both traits Father sanctions fervently.

The second part of his new moniker is more obscure but no less fitting.

Ki. gal; a long-extinct Sumerian term for *underworld* not used since the ancient Mesopotamian period. It is perfect, it literally translates to *knight of night. And besides*, he thinks to himself, *it rolls off the tongue quite nicely.*

He slides vintage Plano eyeglasses onto the bridge of his new nose; these eyes are a bit unnerving, he admits, as he inspects his mirror image. They will take some getting used to.

The glasses are nothing more than a prop, but a rather refined embellishment. They complete the persona, Geoffroi de Kigal, a distinguished scholar from the Department of Education and Research, southeast quadrant.

Father appears in that way he has of moving like a spectra, soundless and surreptitious. Vlad jumps at his manifestation in the background of the mirror, standing at his shoulder. Father quirks a brow at his edgy reaction.

"My Lord," he takes a knee. "You startled me."

"Clearly," Father says somewhat blithely. "Acclimating to your new identity I see."

"Yes, my Lord."

Father does not seek an opinion or approval; Vlad knows better than to offer one.

"Rise." And then, "I assume you have created an alias and supporting backstory, ensuring it rings with authenticity."

"I have my Lord."

"Then let us not tarry. We have work to do."

Pedro hugs his mother again, feeling her silent wailing; the short, stunted heaving of her frame as he pulls her in close. His father stands stout and resolute in contrast to her tormented keening.

"Gina," he says firmly. "It is time. He is a man now; he must make his own way."

He shakes his head and adds, half to himself, "This is not ancient times."

Of course, his father is referring to the cringe-worthy phenomenon that swept society before the Correction. Progeny grown well into adulthood, living in childhood bedrooms or in their parents' basements. Forcibly constrained by a combination of asinine, self-serving, short-sighted government policy and corporate exploits, moving the goal line for the general population from success to survival.

"*Eu sei*," she heaves a great sigh, collecting herself. "I know."

"*Minha mãe*," Pedro speaks softly to his mother, "I will be back, you will once again grow tired of seeing my face!"

His mother shakes her head furiously, the bun low on the back of her head coming loose, her ample cheeks flapping like the jowls of a basset hound. She waggles a finger playfully in front of her son's face.

"*Não* Pedro, I will never grow tired of this face!"

She takes his head between her hands, pulls him to her and kisses his forehead.

Pedro's father eyes his backpack critically.

"Are you certain you have packed everything you will need, son?"

"*Si, Papa*, I have no need for creature comforts. Besides, I will be back before you know it!"

He looks buoyantly at his mother, her face brightening instantly at his words.

"And what of your existing studies? Surely, the *universidade* will struggle in your absence," his mother tries one more time to sway him, his father giving her a warning look under hooded brows.

"Ah *mãe*, my colleagues will be fine without me. I have been afield before, they will adapt," Pedro downplays the magnitude of his self-elected sabbatical.

With the loss of his right arm from *a terrible crush injury* from a rockslide at the Ceará monitoring station and his most recent brush with death as a result of a *faulty interlock* in the northwest apiary compound, no one questioned him when he had announced his furlough. Little do they know that this is anything but a vacation.

José Castillo lends a hand from the grave. As the venerated professor's protegé, the *Universidade Sudoeste Biodoma* approves Pedro's request without question. Keys in hand, he heads to the back lot where a fleet of identical yellow jeeps are lined up like an infantry battalion ready to march.

Number 451 waits for him partway down the line. A queasiness washes over him remembering his last ride in an overland vehicle, although these are austere in comparison to Draeger's behemoth ground-eater.

Pedro was deliberately vague on the return date, feigning weariness when asked. The university administrative agent had nodded her head sympathetically and produced a temporary use permit without pressing further. Being maimed definitely has its advantages.

He places the permit in the window of the jeep, tosses his backpack on the passenger seat and starts the engine. Easing the off-road vehicle out of the parking lot, he watches the education and research complex in the rearview mirror, overwhelmed by a torrent of emotions. He's convinced everyone, his family, his friends and colleagues, even himself, that he will return.

To them, he needs to recharge his batteries. In truth, he needs to accomplish his mission and then, yes, of course, he will settle back into his role in research and education. Denying himself the feeling of estrangement that has been haunting him ever since his return, he smothers the voices in his head urging him to heed the unrelenting sentiment.

Hours pass behind the wheel, compunction creeping over him with each mile. What if he is not well received? Or not received at all? Did he really think this through? Is he making a mistake? Should he turn around and approach his mission from another angle? He grips the steering wheel and bears down on his shoulders. No, he will stay the course, for better or worse.

Dusk is just settling in over the land when he parks the jeep where the road comes to an abrupt end. He sets on foot for the remainder of his journey. Fireflies frolic in the cooling air, an orchestra of night sounds coming to life overhead and underfoot along the overgrown trail, as if announcing his arrival.

He takes his time, savoring the surroundings, shoring up his courage as he follows the indistinct pathway more from memory than from any obvious trail markers. His heart beats in double time as he pushes through the last of the brush and steps into the clearing, clutching the straps of his backpack.

The villagers are gathered around a blazing fire, in full ceremonial dress. A sacred fire then, Pedro realizes, a gateway to the spirit world. The din of conversation ceases, all eyes shifting toward his fixed form in the shadow of the dancing flames. Time stands still.

Tank is the first to move, bounding toward him, digging one-inch claws into the earth as he propels himself forward. The bull mastiff slows his approach, creeping in low, sniffing, assessing. Pedro stands stock-still, waiting for the verdict. The dog lifts his giant head and meets his eyes. And then his tail whips back and forth as he assumes the play bow, chest on the ground, butt in the air.

"Tank, no!" Wandering Tree howls from the circle of light around the fire.

Too late. The dog bowls into Pedro's chest, knocking him backwards. He stumbles, loses his footing and plants his rump none too gently in the grass.

Tank proceeds to climb on his chest and wash his face in copious amounts of slobber, his tongue reaching into every orifice; nose, ears, mouth. Pedro laughs hysterically although it is truly difficult to breathe with one hundred and twenty pounds standing on his chest drowning him in drool.

"*Salto*," the heel command is firm and the dog retreats to sit at his master's side.

Wandering Tree extends an oversized hand to Pedro and lifts him to his feet as easily as picking up a twig. He looks him over, and then takes Pedro into a bear hug that has him once again gasping for air, his face compressed against the giant's torso.

"*Mão Roubada!*" his voice booms, initiating a flurry of chatter from the assembled tribespeople.

One tribe member breaks away from the group and ambles toward Pedro and Wandering Tree, leaning heavily on a walking stick with every second step.

"Where have you been?" Wandering Tree inquires. "We all thought you were gone for good."

Before Pedro can answer the question, Walks in the Rain stands before him. The medicine man lifts his chin with his walking stick, going rigid when he makes contact with Pedro's face. He takes a step back.

"*Anda na Chuva*," Pedro addresses the medicine man by his proper name.

Wandering Tree and Tank are all but forgotten for the moment. His fate will be decided by the old man before him. Walks in the Rain seems to be considering. His face goes slack, a faraway look as his eyes scan the night sky, as if consulting the stars.

He closes them now and hums almost imperceptibly deep in his throat. Pedro feels the weight of the entire village on him, all waiting on bated breath, the only sound from the crackling of burning logs. The tribe elder turns to the fire, addressing the clan.

"Through our sacred fire, this night we receive a gift from the Great Spirit, *o Criador*."

He takes Pedro by the hand and hobbles back to the fire, using his walking stick like a crutch in the other hand. Tank and Wandering Tree follow a few paces behind them, all the exuberance of moments earlier replaced with solemnity.

Pedro averts his eyes, so self-conscious he wants to crawl under a rock. Walks in the Rain's announcement has everyone mystified, himself included. It is only a handful of steps to the fire, but it feels like an eternity.

The old man clears up the mystery with a simple statement, "*Mão Roubada. Santo guerreiro entre nós.*"

He drops Pedro's hand and walks to his clan, turns and faces the entire village and repeats the message.

"Stolen Hand. Holy warrior among us."

The firekeeper adds more fuel, the flames licking higher into the air, a plume of sparks rising up, there and gone like a firecracker.

Red face paint, kohl-lined eyes, a heavy, oversize headdress, black raven feather earrings and matching armbands, bear claw necklace, long grass skirt cinched at the waist with row upon row of intricate black and white beading, barefoot with ankles bound in thick leather bindings…she looks every part the chieftess that she is. Commanding and fierce. Graceful and beautiful. Pedro's breath is swept away like sand on a rising tide.

The rhythmic sound of percussion starts, echoing softly in the night air, quiet and calm as a sleeping heartbeat. As more drums are added, the tempo and intensity grow in tandem. Dancers begin to move around the fire, hypnotic and lithe, weaving a tale without words.

The dance becomes increasingly riveting as the drummers pound faster and faster in perfect synchronicity, the performers stepping and swaying and twisting and careening with inebriating fervency.

Pedro is so mesmerized by the exhibition that he doesn't notice the body that slides in next to him until the feeling of being watched overwhelms him and he forces himself to shift his gaze to his left.

"It is for you," she says with a hint of awe in her voice. "The Warrior Dance."

She proceeds to explain the scenes of the performance.

"The champion is sent to protect mankind, a great battle ensues, he slays the dragon, he returns home victorious."

He feels a rush of adrenaline. So close. As he stares at her, the powerful chieftess disappears, replaced with Morning Sun, the girl, her eyes searching his, hoping not for the holy warrior, but for the boy.

Fragments of the disaffection and alienation that have been plaguing him since his return from the garden begin to fall away at the margins. He doesn't say a word, just stares into Morning Sun's perfect face while the feelings crumble to dust, his heart, his mind, his soul, unchained. She holds his stare, patient, searching for an answer. The same one he has been seeking. Now he has it.

"*Si*, I am home."

Chapter 24

'There are thousands of Himmlers living among us.'
—Erich Fromm, The Anatomy of Human Destructiveness

Vlad's role in the new plan is more central than ever. Father cannot resurrect his earthly form without his assistance. And without the *tetradophobis amplectus*, Father is trapped here, in the Abyss. This simply will not do.

The task is quite elementary really, in theory anyway. The lifeforce of the serpentine manifestation is good old-fashioned, tried-and-true *sin*. Geoffroi de Kigal will nurture man's most basic instinct like a mother tends to her child, with gentle but relentless persuasion. He will bend them to his will.

The existential virus certainly presents an intransigent obstacle, however, as Father explicated rhetorically, why would the Other bother with the virus if the potential for sin were not alive and well? Nothing more than a suppression device, Father had tut-tutted, the virus might deter, but it will never extinguish. It is up to Vlad to find ways to rekindle the flame, one corruptible heart at a time.

Vlad exchanges his trademark three-piece suit and silk tie for an equally stylish grey ribbed cashmere turtleneck tucked into cream-colored Milano pants and belted with a slim silver-buckled black leather belt and tied together with matching black penny loafers.

The chic glasses and edgy but expertly coiffed side-swept hair complete the persona of the ever capable, uber intelligent, Geoffroi de Kigal. Time to make his debut, the Biodome is waiting. And he has a few scores to settle.

When Maureen finalizes the dismantling of Draeger's administration, the handshakes and farewells of her co-cabinet members as they scatter back to their respective departments in their respective quadrants in her rearview mirror, she takes a minute to breathe it all in.

The weight of a thousand suns lifts from her shoulders, the dirty, roiling clouds hanging over her conscience thin to dull wisps carried away on a cleansing breeze. She's not sure she will ever come to terms with Jacob, never knowing the truth, but at least she's done one thing right. Oddly, she takes comfort in knowing her son would be proud of her.

She shivers at the thought of Draeger, his final moments, his fall from grace, his demise. The room, the pit, the smell…the missing body. This keeps her up at night. Most mornings at the breakfast table, Peter asks what has her jumping in her sleep.

She will never, ever tell. Sandra Steele is the only person she has talked to about what she witnessed, the only person who understands that Dr. Draeger was not who he pretended to be. That he was so, so much more. Even then, the two women stopped short of pursuing the matter, making a pact never to speak of it again.

She absentmindedly begins unpacking boxes, needing to do something with her hands to get out of her own head. She destroyed most of the cabinet's records back at headquarters, seeing no need to retain all those spurious reports, all that misrepresented data, all the fraudulent schemes and plans.

They serve no purpose other than to remind her of her part in Draeger's wicked games. She is appalled with herself for resorting to the ancient bureaucratic method, shredding the evidence, hiding the truth. But alas, there is nought to be done for it now.

Her DHP office is like an old friend, it welcomes her home with open arms, no questions asked. There is one addition to her finely polished desk though. She carefully sets down a framed photo of Jacob, smiling ear to ear, kneeling beside his great German Shepperd, Hercules, the dog as happy as the boy. Peter snapped the pic on his cell phone the week before Jacob disappeared.

He'd had it printed and framed and placed it at the end of the photo journey on the side table in the family room. Jacob as an infant in his crib, an open-mouthed one-year-old in a bouncer, three in his first plastic car, a toothless six-year-old in the sandbox, all the stages of childhood into his teens and culminating in this last photo of a grown man.

Peter can replace it; she needs this one beside her. She swallows, a lump forming in her throat. She wears her regret like a scarf wound too tight around her neck.

"I am so very sorry, Jacob," she says to the framed image. "It is all so clear to me now."

She huffs a big sigh and sets to acquainting herself with current health promotion projects in her district. Gone are the days of violence prevention, substance abuse and gambling programs, EV took care of a myriad of self-destructive behaviors long ago. But there is still much to be done.

She nods approvingly at a new district-wide program aimed at engaging youth in the art of backyard gardening with the department of agriculture, another community walking club for seniors with the department of elder care, a multitude of simple yet incredibly effective wellness initiatives, something for everyone. Her name appears as the lead agent responsible for program oversight on every project except for one. It grabs her attention.

A study more than a program, investigating the effects of the recent turmoil caused by Dr. Vladimir Draeger on the health and mental well-being of the Biodome citizenry. Dangerous territory. Why here, in Midwest HP? And to what end, she wonders.

She is instantly irritated, she wants nothing more than to put that chapter to rest, permanently. She cannot fathom what the Biodome hopes to achieve by dredging up the events of the past months.

She makes a note to speak directly with the lead agent, noting he is scheduled to arrive tomorrow morning. Hailing from the Department of Research and Education, he is coming all the way from his home base in the southeast quadrant to manage this ostensibly nugatory endeavor. Her eyebrows disappear into her hairline as she reads the lead agent's name. Geoffroi de Kigal.

On a rocky mountain pass, a dark grey puddle, like dried concrete, stains the landscape. A ubiquitous calm envelops the ridge and surrounding foothills. The wind heaves a sigh of relief, forbearing as it sails languorously through the pass.

A family of prairie dogs is diligently burrowing away, the litter of four curious pups work alongside mom, taking turns popping up on hind legs to survey the horizon, a lively game of whack a mole.

A herd of mule deer stroll into the thoroughfare, examining the scrubby vegetation as they make their way over to the other side, in no hurry. They track the colorful mountain bluebirds as they flit from branch to branch on the threadbare trees that cling to the gritty soil. They all give a wide berth to the unnatural blot of grey stone, the only scar from the epic battle that fomented in this pass just a few short months ago.

The garden is recovering inch by inch, minute by minute. Each new leaf that unfurls, every cub born, every inlet, every waterway restored, one step closer to redressing the heinous trespasses.

The Chosen One, the girl, the warrior, the wolf, all gone, but not forgotten. No, never forgotten. That they've left the site of the siege without so much as an afterthought is a blessing in disguise. He's left in peace, biding his time.

Vlad is busy indeed, wily as ever. Drawing out a little fib here, a little boasting there, ferrets out some perfidious intentions, facilitating some trivial pilfering, some extramarital philandering, it's all adding up. Man cannot help himself, virus or no virus. So long as Vlad remains steadfast in his goading, it will be enough. This redemption will be short-lived.

A faint rustling sound tickles the air. The prairie dogs stop digging, ears twitching, moving as one in the direction of the muffled noise. The deer mimic, losing interest in the twigs and scrub. Watching. Waiting.

From a deep crevice between the base of the eastward-facing slope and a jagged boulder sheared from the face of the mountain; a small object rolls leisurely out into the open pass. The deer scatter, the ingenuous rodents dive into their hard-won warrens, pretty little birds take flight on Hagrid wings.

One more half-turn and the anamorphic orb comes to rest, losing a ribbed, translucent layer on the last rotation. The garden goes silent and still, holding its breath as two bottomless gilded eyes, perfectly bisected by slits as black as a moonless night stare up into the deep blue sky, a single lash of forked tongue tasting the air, scenting the wind. Heady and strong. Exquisite. Unassailable. Fear.

Epilogue

My third warrior surprised me with his return. But the boy does not squander his gift; he learns, he grows, he becomes. He chose his teacher well; the Tupi wise man is patient and munificent with his knowledge, his connection to the truth deep and visceral.

Owing to the tutelage, combined with his unwavering faith, the boy's heart and mind open a little more each day, thinning the veil between realms.

It has not escaped me that I find myself sharing his affections with another, her strength and beauty, her virtue, worthy of him. I approve. Despite the sacramental burden he must continue to carry, he deserves true love and unbridled happiness.

The same love that Chosen One and Little Lionheart share. When they knelt before me on the bank of the creek, hand-in-hand, asking me to bless their union, I did so without reservation. I alone, and I suppose the wolf, bore witness. No theatrics, no pomp and circumstance. They were joined in a way that transcends the meretricious ceremony. Their bond will endure, for all time.

Redemption on Earth. Already His spawn chips away at the foundation of your hard-won freedom. Enslaves you all over again, one anodyne sin at a time. Grooming you, lulling you into a false sense of security. I will concede, He is cunning.

I have weaponized the Biodome to ensure that consequences are commensurate with the crime. At this rate, He will have succeeded in precipitating a global pandemic in no time. Countless relatively mild transgressions with relatively mild repercussions. Just enough to resurrect His earthly form. To release Him from eternal captivity.

And so, we will start all over again. All because you would barter your corporal health and pervert your spiritual well-being, tolerate the discomforts of illness in exchange for exercising your free will. To misbehave. To disobey.

To sin. Even now, as I speak, the esophagus and tracheal lung are forming and his brain function is fully restored.

You simply refuse to learn.

Very well then, I have my sedulous triad. They will not fail me.

But wait. I err.

Well met, my dearest Empress, you serve me well.

Where two purest hearts beat in the shade of the Tree of Life, now there are three.